7 BEST SHORT STORIES
WESTERN

TACET BOOKS

7 BEST SHORT STORIES
WESTERN

EDITED BY
AUGUST NEMO

EDITOR August Nemo
COVER AND INTERIOR DESIGN Mayra Falcini
MARKETING Horacio Corral

Publisher's Cataloging-In-Publication Data (CIP)

Nemo, August (org.)
N436   7 best short stories - Western / August Nemo (org.) –
São Paulo, SP: Tacet Books, 2021.
129 p. 14 x 21 cm

ISBN 978-65-89575-19-1

1. American Literature in English.

                                        CDD 810

TACET BOOKS
Made in silence
For noisy minds

www.tacetbooks.com
tacet.books@gmail.com

CONTENTS

INTRODUCTION

Western, a genre of novels and short stories, motion pictures, and television and radio shows that are set in the American West, usually in the period from the 1850s to the end of the 19th century. Though basically an American creation, the western had its counterparts in the gaucho literature of Argentina and in tales of the settlement of the Australian outback. The genre reached its greatest popularity in the early and middle decades of the 20th century and declined somewhat thereafter.

The western has as its setting the immense plains, rugged tablelands, and mountain ranges of the portion of the United States lying west of the Mississippi River, in particular the Great Plains and the Southwest. This area was not truly opened to white settlement until after the American Civil War (1861-65), at which time the Plains Indians were gradually subdued and deprived of most of their lands by white settlers and by the U.S. cavalry. The conflict between white pioneers and Indians forms one of the basic themes of the western. Another sprang out of the class of men known as cowboys, who were hired by ranchers to drive cattle across hundreds of miles of Western pasturelands to railheads where the animals could be shipped eastward to market. The cattle and mining industries spurred the growth of towns, and the gradual imposition of law and order that such settled communities needed was accomplished by another class of men who became staple figures in the western, the town sheriff and the U.S. marshal. Actual historical persons in the American West have figured prominently in latter-day re-creations of the era. Wild Bill Hickok, Wyatt Earp, and other lawmen have frequently been portrayed, as have such outlaws as Billy the Kid and Jesse James.

The western has always provided a rich mine for stories of adventure, and indeed a huge number of purely commercial works have capitalized on the basic appeal of gunslinging frontier adventurers, desperadoes, and lawmen. But the western has also furnished the material for a higher form of artistic vehicle, particularly in motion pictures. This was perhaps because the historical western setting lacked the subtly confining web of social conventions and mundane safeties that typify more settled societies. The West's tenuous hold on the rule of law and its fluid social fabric necessitated the settling of individual and group conflicts by the use of violence and the exercise of physical courage, and the moral dramas and dilemmas arising within this elemental, even primeval, framework lent themselves remarkably well to motion-picture treatment.

In literature the western story had its beginnings in the first adventure narratives that accompanied the opening of the West to white settlement shortly before the Civil War. Accounts of the Western plainsmen, scouts, buffalo hunters, and trappers were highly popular in the East. Perhaps the earliest and finest work in this genre was James Fenimore Cooper's The Prairie (1827), though the high artistic level of this novel was perhaps atypical in regard to what followed. An early writer to capitalize on the popularity of western adventure narratives was E.Z.C. Judson, whose pseudonym was Ned Buntline; known as "the father of the dime novel," he wrote dozens of western stories and was responsible for transforming Buffalo Bill into an archetype. Owen Wister, who first saw the West while recuperating from an illness, wrote the first western that won critical praise, The Virginian (1902). Classics of the genre have been written by men who actually worked as cowboys; one of the best loved of these was Bransford in Arcadia (1914; reprinted 1917 as Bransford of Rainbow Range) by Eugene Manlove Rhodes, a former cowboy and government scout. Andy Adams incorporated many autobiographical incidents in his Log of a Cowboy (1903). By far the best known and one of the most prolific writers of westerns was Zane Grey, an Ohio dentist who became famous with the classic Riders of the Purple Sage (1912). In all, Grey wrote more than 80 books, many of which retained wide popularity. Another popular and prolific writer of westerns was Louis L'Amour.

Western short stories have also been among America's favourites. A.H. Lewis (c. 1858-1914), a former cowboy, produced a series of popular stories told by the "Old Cattleman." Stephen Crane created a comic classic of the genre with "The Bride Comes to Yellow Sky" (1898), and Conrad Richter (1890-1968) wrote a number of stories and novels of the Old Southwest. The Western Writers of America, formed in 1952, has cited many fine western writers, including Ernest Haycox (1899-1950); W.M. Raine (1871-1954), a former Arizona ranger who wrote more than 80 western novels; and B.M. Bower (1871-1940), a woman whose talent for realistic detail convinced thousands of readers that she was a real cowboy writing from personal experience. Other western classics are Walter van Tilburg Clark's The Ox-Bow Incident (1940), which uses a Nevada lynching as a metaphor for the struggle for justice; A.B. Guthrie, Jr.'s The Big Sky (1947), about frontier life in the early 1840s, and The Way West (1949); and Larry McMurtry's Pulitzer Prize-winning paean to the bygone cowboy, Lonesome Dove (1985). Many western novels and short stories first appeared in pulp magazines, such as Ace-High Western Stories and Double Action Western, that were specifically devoted to publishing works in the genre.

THE OUTCASTS OF POKER FLAT

Bret Harte

As Mr. John Oakhurst, gambler, stepped into the main street of Poker Flat on the morning of the twenty-third of November, 1850, he was conscious of a change in its moral atmosphere since the preceding night. Two or three men, conversing earnestly together, ceased as he approached, and exchanged significant glances. There was a Sabbath lull in the air which, in a settlement unused to Sabbath influences, looked ominous.

Mr. Oakhurst's calm, handsome face betrayed small concern in these indications. Whether he was conscious of any predisposing cause was another question. "I reckon they're after somebody," he reflected; "likely it's me." He returned to his pocket the handkerchief with which he had been whipping away the red dust of Poker Flat from his neat boots, and quietly discharged his mind of any further conjecture.

In point of fact, Poker Flat was "after somebody." It had lately suffered the loss of several thousand dollars, two valuable horses, and a prominent citizen. It was experiencing a spasm of virtuous reaction, quite as lawless and ungovernable as any of the acts that had provoked it. A secret committee had determined to rid the town of all improper persons. This was done permanently in regard of two men who were then hanging from the boughs of a sycamore in the gulch, and temporarily in the banishment of certain other objectionable characters. I regret to say that some of these were ladies. It is but due to the sex, however, to state that their impropriety was professional, and it was only in such easily established standards of evil that Poker Flat ventured to sit in judgment.

Mr. Oakhurst was right in supposing that he was included in this category. A few of the committee had urged hanging him as a possible example, and a sure method of reimbursing themselves from his pockets of the sums he had won from them. "It's agin justice," said Jim Wheeler, "to let this yer young man from Roaring Camp-an entire stranger-carry away our money." But a crude sentiment of equity residing in the breasts of those who had been fortunate enough to win from Mr. Oakhurst overruled this narrower local prejudice.

Mr. Oakhurst received his sentence with philosophic calmness, none the less coolly that he was aware of the hesitation of his judges. He was too much of a gambler not to accept Fate. With him life was at best an uncertain game, and he recognized the usual percentage in favor of the dealer.

A body of armed men accompanied the deported wickedness of Poker Flat to the outskirts of the settlement. Besides Mr. Oakhurst, who was known to be a coolly desperate man, and for whose intimidation the armed escort was intended, the expatriated party consisted of a young woman familiarly known as the "Duchess"; another, who had won the title of "Mother Shipton"; and "Uncle Billy," a suspected sluice-robber and confirmed drunkard. The cavalcade provoked no comments from the spectators, nor was any word uttered by the escort. Only, when the gulch which marked the uttermost limit of Poker Flat was reached, the leader spoke briefly and to the point. The exiles were forbidden to return at the peril of their lives.

As the escort disappeared, their pent-up feelings found vent in a few hysterical tears from the Duchess, some bad language from Mother Shipton, and a Parthian volley of expletives from Uncle Billy. The philosophic Oakhurst alone remained silent. He listened calmly to Mother Shipton's desire to cut somebody's heart out, to the repeated statements of the Duchess that she would die in the road, and to the alarming oaths that seemed to be bumped out of Uncle Billy as he rode forward. With the easy good humor characteristic of his class, he insisted upon exchanging his own riding horse, "Five Spot," for the sorry mule which the Duchess rode. But even this act did not draw the party into any closer sympathy. The young woman readjusted her somewhat draggled plumes with a feeble, faded coquetry; Mother Shipton eyed the possessor of "Five Spot" with malevolence, and Uncle Billy included the whole party in one sweeping anathema.

The road to Sandy Bar-a camp that, not having as yet experienced the regenerating influences of Poker Flat, consequently seemed to offer some invitation to the emigrants-lay over a steep mountain range. It was distant a day's severe travel. In that advanced season, the party soon passed out of the moist, temperate regions of the foothills into the dry, cold, bracing air of the Sierras. The trail was narrow and difficult. At noon the Duchess, rolling out of her saddle upon the ground, declared her intention of going no farther, and the party halted.

The spot was singularly wild and impressive. A wooded amphitheater, surrounded on three sides by precipitous cliffs of naked granite, sloped gently toward the crest of another precipice that overlooked the valley. It was, undoubtedly, the most suitable spot for a camp, had camping been advisable. But Mr. Oakhurst knew that scarcely half the journey to Sandy Bar was accomplished, and the party were not equipped or provisioned for delay. This fact he pointed out to his companions curtly, with a philosophic commentary on the folly of "throwing up their hand before the game was played out." But they were furnished with liquor, which in this emergency stood them in place of food, fuel, rest, and prescience. In spite of his remonstrances, it was not long before they were more or less under its influence. Uncle Billy passed rapidly from a bellicose state into one of stupor, the Duchess became maudlin, and Mother Shipton snored. Mr. Oakhurst alone remained erect, leaning against a rock, calmly surveying them.

Mr. Oakhurst did not drink. It interfered with a profession which required coolness, impassiveness, and presence of mind, and, in his own language, he "couldn't afford it." As he gazed at his recumbent fellow exiles, the loneliness begotten of his pariah trade, his habits of life, his very vices, for the first time seriously oppressed him. He bestirred himself in dusting his black clothes, washing his hands and face, and other acts characteristic of his studiously neat habits, and for a moment forgot his annoyance. The thought of deserting his weaker and more pitiable companions never perhaps occurred to him. Yet he could not help feeling the want of that excitement which, singularly enough, was most conducive to that calm equanimity for which he was notorious. He looked at the gloomy walls that rose a thousand feet sheer above the circling pines around him; at the sky, ominously clouded; at the valley below, already deepening into shadow. And, doing so, suddenly he heard his own name called.

A horseman slowly ascended the trail. In the fresh, open face of the newcomer Mr. Oakhurst recognized Tom Simson, otherwise known as the "Innocent" of Sandy Bar. He had met him some months before over a "little game," and had, with perfect equanimity, won the entire fortune-amounting to some forty dollars-of that guileless youth. After the game was finished, Mr. Oakhurst drew the youthful speculator behind the door and thus addressed him: "Tommy, you're a good little man, but you can't gamble worth a cent. Don't try it over again." He then handed him his money back, pushed him gently from the room, and so made a devoted slave of Tom Simson.

There was a remembrance of this in his boyish and enthusiastic greeting of Mr. Oakhurst. He had started, he said, to go to Poker Flat to seek his fortune. "Alone?" No, not exactly alone; in fact (a giggle), he had run away with Piney Woods. Didn't Mr. Oakhurst remember Piney? She that used to wait on the table at the Temperance House? They had been engaged a long time, but old Jake Woods had objected, and so they had run away, and were going to Poker Flat to be married, and here they were. And they were tired out, and how lucky it was they had found a place to camp and company. All this the Innocent delivered rapidly, while Piney, a stout, comely damsel of fifteen, emerged from behind the pine tree, where she had been blushing unseen, and rode to the side of her lover.

Mr. Oakhurst seldom troubled himself with sentiment, still less with propriety; but he had a vague idea that the situation was not fortunate. He retained, however, his presence of mind sufficiently to kick Uncle Billy, who was about to say something, and Uncle Billy was sober enough to recognize in Mr. Oakhurst's kick a superior power that would not bear trifling. He then endeavored to dissuade Tom Simson from delaying further, but in vain. He even pointed out the fact that there was no provision, nor means of making a camp. But, unluckily, the Innocent met this objection by assuring the party that he was provided with an extra mule loaded with provisions and by the discovery of a rude attempt at a log house near the trail. "Piney can stay with Mrs. Oakhurst," said the Innocent, pointing to the Duchess, "and I can shift for myself."

Nothing but Mr. Oakhurst's admonishing foot saved Uncle Billy from bursting into a roar of laughter. As it was, he felt compelled to retire up the canyon until he could recover his gravity. There he confided the joke to the tall pine trees, with many slaps of his leg, contortions of his face, and the usual profanity. But when he returned to the party, he found them seated by a fire-for the air had grown strangely chill and the sky overcast-in apparently amicable conversation. Piney was actually talking in an impulsive, girlish fashion to the Duchess, who was listening with an interest and animation she had not shown for many days. The Innocent was holding forth, apparently with equal effect, to Mr. Oakhurst and Mother Shipton, who was actually relaxing into amiability. "Is this yer a damned picnic?" said Uncle Billy with inward scorn as he surveyed the sylvan group, the glancing firelight, and the tethered animals in the foreground. Suddenly an idea mingled with the alcoholic fumes that disturbed his brain. It was apparently of a jocular nature, for he felt impelled to slap his leg again and cram his fist into his mouth.

As the shadows crept slowly up the mountain, a slight breeze rocked the tops of the pine trees, and moaned through their long and gloomy aisles. The ruined cabin, patched and covered with pine boughs, was set apart for the ladies. As the lovers parted, they unaffectedly exchanged a kiss, so honest and sincere that it might have been heard above the swaying pines. The frail Duchess and the malevolent Mother Shipton were probably too stunned to remark upon this last evidence of simplicity, and so turned without a word to the hut. The fire was replenished, the men lay down before the door, and in a few minutes were asleep.

Mr. Oakhurst was a light sleeper. Toward morning he awoke benumbed and cold. As he stirred the dying fire, the wind, which was now blowing strongly, brought to his cheek that which caused the blood to leave it-snow!

He started to his feet with the intention of awakening the sleepers, for there was no time to lose. But turning to where Uncle Billy had been lying, he found him gone. A suspicion leaped to his brain and a curse to his lips. He ran to the spot where the mules had been tethered; they were no longer there. The tracks were already rapidly disappearing in the snow.

The momentary excitement brought Mr. Oakhurst back to the fire with his usual calm. He did not waken the sleepers. The Innocent slumbered peacefully, with a smile on his good-humored, freckled face; the virgin Piney slept beside her frailer sisters as sweetly as though attended by celestial guardians; and Mr. Oakhurst, drawing his blanket over his shoulders, stroked his mustaches and waited for the dawn. It came slowly in a whirling mist of snowflakes that dazzled and confused the eye. What could be seen of the landscape appeared magically changed. He looked over the valley, and summed up the present and future in two words-"snowed in!"

A careful inventory of the provisions, which, fortunately for the party, had been stored within the hut and so escaped the felonious fingers of Uncle Billy, disclosed the fact that with care and prudence they might last ten days longer. "That is," said Mr. Oakhurst, sotto voce to the Innocent, "if you're willing to board us. If you ain't-and perhaps you'd better not-you can wait till Uncle Billy gets back with provisions." For some occult reason, Mr. Oakhurst could not bring himself to disclose Uncle Billy's rascality, and so offered the hypothesis that he had wandered from the camp and had accidentally stampeded the animals. He dropped a warning to the Duchess and Mother Shipton, who of course knew the facts of their associate's defection. "They'll find out the truth about us all when they find out anything," he added, significantly, "and there's no good frightening them now."

Tom Simson not only put all his worldly store at the disposal of Mr. Oakhurst, but seemed to enjoy the prospect of their enforced seclusion. "We'll have a good camp for a week, and then the snow'll melt, and we'll all go back together." The cheerful gaiety of the young man, and Mr. Oakhurst's calm, infected the others. The Innocent with the aid of pine boughs extemporized a thatch for the roofless cabin, and the Duchess directed Piney in the rearrangement of the interior with a taste and tact that opened the blue eyes of that provincial maiden to their fullest extent.

"I reckon now you're used to fine things at Poker Flat," said Piney. The Duchess turned away sharply to conceal something that reddened her cheeks through its professional tint, and Mother Shipton requested Piney not to "chatter." But when Mr. Oakhurst returned from a weary search for the trail, he heard the sound of happy laughter echoed from the rocks. He stopped in some alarm, and his thoughts first naturally reverted to the whisky, which he had prudently cached. "And yet it don't somehow sound like whisky," said the gambler. It was not until he caught sight of the blazing fire through the still-blinding storm and the group around it that he settled to the conviction that it was "square fun."

Whether Mr. Oakhurst had cached his cards with the whisky as something debarred the free access of the community, I cannot say. It was certain that, in Mother Shipton's words, he "didn't say cards once" during that evening. Haply the time was beguiled by an accordion, produced somewhat ostentatiously by Tom Simson from his pack. Notwithstanding some difficulties attending the manipulation of this instrument, Piney Woods managed to pluck several reluctant melodies from its keys, to an accompaniment by the Innocent on a pair of bone castanets. But the crowning festivity of the evening was reached in a rude camp-meeting hymn, which the lovers, joining hands, sang with great earnestness and vociferation. I fear that a certain defiant tone and Covenanter's swing to its chorus, rather than any devotional quality, caused it speedily to infect the others, who at last joined in the refrain:

"I'm proud to live in the service of the Lord,
And I'm bound to die in His army."

The pines rocked, the storm eddied and whirled above the miserable group, and the flames of their altar leaped heavenward as if in token of the vow.

At midnight the storm abated, the rolling clouds parted, and the stars glittered keenly above the sleeping camp. Mr. Oakhurst, whose professional habits had enabled him to live on the smallest possible amount of sleep, in dividing the watch with Tom Simson somehow managed to take upon himself the greater part of that duty. He excused himself to the Innocent by saying that he had "often been a week without sleep." "Doing what?" asked Tom. "Poker!" replied Oakhurst, sententiously; "when a man gets a streak of luck,-nigger luck-he don't get tired. The luck gives in first. Luck," continued the gambler, reflectively, "is a mighty queer thing. All you know about it for certain is that it's bound to change. And it's finding out when it's going to change that makes you. We've had a streak of bad luck since we left Poker Flat-you come along, and slap you get into it, too. If you can hold your cards right along you're all right. For," added the gambler, with cheerful irrelevance,

"'I'm proud to live in the service of the Lord,
And I'm bound to die in His army.'"

The third day came, and the sun, looking through the white- curtained valley, saw the outcasts divide their slowly decreasing store of provisions for the morning meal. It was one of the peculiarities of that mountain climate that its rays diffused a kindly warmth over the wintry landscape, as if in regretful commiseration of the past. But it revealed drift on drift of snow piled high around the hut-a hopeless, uncharted, trackless sea of white lying below the rocky shores to which the castaways still clung. Through the marvelously clear air the smoke of the pastoral village of Poker Flat rose miles away. Mother Shipton saw it, and from a remote pinnacle of her rocky fastness hurled in that direction a final malediction. It was her last vituperative attempt, and perhaps for that reason was invested with a certain degree of sublimity. It did her good, she privately informed the Duchess. "Just you go out there and cuss, and see." She then set herself to the task of amusing "the child," as she and the Duchess were pleased to call Piney. Piney was no chicken, but it was a soothing and original theory of the pair thus to account for the fact that she didn't swear and wasn't improper.

When night crept up again through the gorges, the reedy notes of the accordion rose and fell in fitful spasms and long-drawn gasps by the flickering campfire. But music failed to fill entirely the aching void left by insufficient food, and a new diversion was proposed by Piney-storytelling. Neither Mr. Oakhurst nor his female companions caring to relate their personal experiences, this plan would have failed too but for the Innocent. Some months before he had chanced upon a stray copy of Mr. Pope's ingenious translation of the ILIAD. He now proposed to narrate the principal incidents of that poem-having thoroughly mastered the argument and fairly forgotten the words-in the current vernacular of Sandy Bar. And so for the rest of that night the Homeric demigods again walked the earth. Trojan bully and wily Greek wrestled in the winds, and the great pines in the canyon seemed to bow to the wrath of the son of Peleus. Mr. Oakhurst listened with quiet satisfaction. Most especially was he interested in the fate of "Ash-heels," as the Innocent persisted in denominating the "swift-footed Achilles."

So with small food and much of Homer and the accordion, a week passed over the heads of the outcasts. The sun again forsook them, and again from leaden skies the snowflakes were sifted over the land. Day by day closer around them drew the snowy circle, until at last they looked from their prison over drifted walls of dazzling white that towered twenty feet above their heads. It became more and more difficult to replenish their fires, even from the fallen trees beside them, now half-hidden in the drifts. And yet no one complained. The lovers turned from the dreary prospect and looked into each other's eyes, and were happy. Mr. Oakhurst settled himself coolly to the losing game before him. The Duchess, more cheerful than she had been, assumed the care of Piney. Only Mother Shipton-once the strongest of the party-seemed to sicken and fade. At midnight on the tenth day she called Oakhurst to her side. "I'm going," she said, in a voice of querulous weakness, "but don't say anything about it. Don't waken the kids. Take the bundle from under my head and open it." Mr. Oakhurst did so. It contained Mother Shipton's rations for the last week, untouched. "Give 'em to the child," she said, pointing to the sleeping Piney. "You've starved yourself," said the gambler. "That's what they call it," said the woman, querulously, as she lay down again and, turning her face to the wall, passed quietly away.

The accordion and the bones were put aside that day, and Homer was forgotten. When the body of Mother Shipton had been committed to the snow, Mr. Oakhurst took the Innocent aside, and showed him a pair of snowshoes, which he had fashioned from the old pack saddle. "There's one chance in a hundred to save her yet," he said, pointing to Piney; "but it's there," he added, pointing toward Poker Flat. "If you can reach there in two days she's safe." "And you?" asked Tom Simson. "I'll stay here," was the curt reply.

The lovers parted with a long embrace. "You are not going, too?" said the Duchess as she saw Mr. Oakhurst apparently waiting to accompany him. "As far as the canyon," he replied. He turned suddenly, and kissed the Duchess, leaving her pallid face aflame and her trembling limbs rigid with amazement.

Night came, but not Mr. Oakhurst. It brought the storm again and the whirling snow. Then the Duchess, feeding the fire, found that someone had quietly piled beside the hut enough fuel to last a few days longer. The tears rose to her eyes, but she hid them from Piney.

The women slept but little. In the morning, looking into each other's faces, they read their fate. Neither spoke; but Piney, accepting the position of the stronger, drew near and placed her arm around the Duchess's waist. They kept this attitude for the rest of the day. That night the storm reached its greatest fury, and, rending asunder the protecting pines, invaded the very hut.

Toward morning they found themselves unable to feed the fire, which gradually died away. As the embers slowly blackened, the Duchess crept closer to Piney, and broke the silence of many hours: "Piney, can you pray?" "No, dear," said Piney, simply. The Duchess, without knowing exactly why, felt relieved, and, putting her head upon Piney's shoulder, spoke no more. And so reclining, the younger and purer pillowing the head of her soiled sister upon her virgin breast, they fell asleep.

The wind lulled as if it feared to waken them. Feathery drifts of snow, shaken from the long pine boughs, flew like white-winged birds, and settled about them as they slept. The moon through the rifted clouds looked down upon what had been the camp. But all human stain, all trace of earthly travail, was hidden beneath the spotless mantle mercifully flung from above.

They slept all that day and the next, nor did they waken when voices and footsteps broke the silence of the camp. And when pitying fingers brushed the snow from their wan faces, you could scarcely have told from the equal peace that dwelt upon them which was she that had sinned. Even the law of Poker Flat recognized this, and turned away, leaving them still locked in each other's arms.

But at the head of the gulch, on one of the largest pine trees, they found the deuce of clubs pinned to the bark with a bowie knife. It bore the following, written in pencil, in a firm hand:

BENEATH THIS TREE
LIES THE BODY
OF
JOHN OAKHURST,
WHO STRUCK A STREAK OF BAD LUCK
ON THE 23D OF NOVEMBER, 1850,
AND
HANDED IN HIS CHECKS
ON THE 7TH DECEMBER, 1850.

And pulseless and cold, with a Derringer by his side and a bullet in his heart, though still calm as in life, beneath the snow lay he who was at once the strongest and yet the weakest of the outcasts of Poker Flat.

ALL GOLD CANYON

Jack London

It was the green heart of the canyon, where the walls
swerved back from the rigid plan and relieved their
harshness of line by making a little sheltered nook and
filling it to the brim with sweetness and roundness and soft-
ness. Here all things rested. Even the narrow stream ceased
its turbulent down-rush long enough to form a quiet pool.
Knee-deep in the water, with drooping head and half-shut
eyes, drowsed a red-coated, many-antlered buck.

On one side, beginning at the very lip of the pool, was a
tiny meadow, a cool, resilient surface of green that extended to the base of the frowning wall. Beyond the pool a gentle slope of earth ran up and up to meet the opposing wall.
Fine grass covered the slope-grass that was spangled with
flowers, with here and there patches of color, orange and
purple and golden. Below, the canyon was shut in. There
was no view. The walls leaned together abruptly and the
canyon ended in a chaos of rocks, moss-covered and hidden
by a green screen of vines and creepers and boughs of trees.
Up the canyon rose far hills and peaks, the big foothills,
pine-covered and remote. And far beyond, like clouds upon
the border of the slay, towered minarets of white, where the
Sierra's eternal snows flashed austerely the blazes of the sun.

There was no dust in the canyon. The leaves and flowers
were clean and virginal. The grass was young velvet. Over
the pool three cottonwoods sent their scurvy fluffs fluttering
down the quiet air. On the slope the blossoms of the wine-
wooded manzanita filled the air with springtime odors, while
the leaves, wise with experience, were already beginning their
vertical twist against the coming aridity of summer. In the
open spaces on the slope, beyond the farthest shadow-reach
of the manzanita, poised the mariposa lilies, like so many
flights of jewelled moths suddenly arrested and on the verge
of trembling into flight again. Here and there that woods
harlequin, the madrone, permitting itself to be caught in the

act of changing its pea-green trunk to madder-red, breathed its fragrance into the air from great clusters of waxen bells. Creamy white were these bells, shaped like lilies-of-the-valley, with the sweetness of perfume that is of the springtime.

There was not a sigh of wind. The air was drowsy with its weight of perfume. It was a sweetness that would have been cloying had the air been heavy and humid. But the air was sharp and thin. It was as starlight transmuted into atmosphere, shot through and warmed by sunshine, and flower-drenched with sweetness.

An occasional butterfly drifted in and out through the patches of light and shade. And from all about rose the low and sleepy hum of mountain bees-feasting Sybarites that jostled one another good-naturedly at the board, nor found time for rough discourtesy. So quietly did the little stream drip and ripple its way through the canyon that it spoke only in faint and occasional gurgles. The voice of the stream was as a drowsy whisper, ever interrupted by dozings and silences, ever lifted again in the awakenings.

The motion of all things was a drifting in the heart of the canyon. Sunshine and butterflies drifted in and out among the trees. The hum of the bees and the whisper of the stream were a drifting of sound. And the drifting sound and drifting color seemed to weave together in the making of a delicate and intangible fabric which was the spirit of the place. It was a spirit of peace that was not of death, but of smooth-pulsing life, of quietude that was not silence, of movement that was not action, of repose that was quick with existence without being violent with struggle and travail. The spirit of the place was the spirit of the peace of the living, somnolent with the easement and content of prosperity, and undisturbed by rumors of far wars.

The red-coated, many-antlered buck acknowledged the lordship of the spirit of the place and dozed knee-deep in the cool, shaded pool. There seemed no flies to vex him and he was languid with rest. Sometimes his ears moved when the stream awoke and whispered; but they moved lazily, with, foreknowledge that it was merely the stream grown garrulous at discovery that it had slept.

But there came a time when the buck's ears lifted and tensed with swift eagerness for sound. His head was turned down the canyon. His sensitive, quivering nostrils scented the air. His eyes could not pierce the green screen through which the stream rippled away, but to his ears came the voice of a man. It was a steady, monotonous, singsong voice. Once the buck heard the harsh clash of metal upon rock. At the sound he snorted with a sudden start that jerked him through the air from water to meadow, and his feet sank into the young velvet, while he pricked his ears and again scented the air. Then he stole across the tiny meadow, pausing once and again to listen, and faded away out of the canyon like a wraith, soft-footed and without sound.

The clash of steel-shod soles against the rocks began to be heard, and the man's voice grew louder. It was raised in a sort of chant and became distinct with nearness, so that the words could be heard:

> *"Turn around an' tu'n yo' face*
> *'Untoe them sweet hills of grace*
> *(D' pow'rs of sin yo' am scornin'!).*
> *Look about an' look aroun',*
> *Fling yo' sin-pack on d' groun'*
> *(Yo' will meet wid d' Lord in d' mornin'!)."*

A sound of scrambling accompanied the song, and the spirit of the place fled away on the heels of the red-coated buck. The green screen was burst asunder, and a man peered out at the meadow and the pool and the sloping side-hill. He was a deliberate sort of man. He took in the scene with one embracing glance, then ran his eyes over the details to verify the general impression. Then, and not until then, did he open his mouth in vivid and solemn approval:

"Smoke of life an' snakes of purgatory! Will you just look at that! Wood an' water an' grass an' a side-hill! A pocket-hunter's delight an' a cayuse's paradise! Cool green for tired eyes! Pink pills for pale people ain't in it. A secret pasture for prospectors and a resting-place for tired burros, by damn!"

He was a sandy-complexioned man in whose face geniality and humor seemed the salient characteristics. It was a mobile face, quick-changing to inward mood and thought. Thinking was in him a visible process. Ideas chased across his face like wind-flaws across the surface of a lake. His hair, sparse and unkempt of growth, was as indeterminate and colorless as his complexion. It would seem that all the color of his frame had gone into his eyes, for they were startlingly blue. Also, they were laughing and merry eyes, within them much of the naivete and wonder of the child; and yet, in an unassertive way, they contained much of calm self-reliance and strength of purpose founded upon self-experience and experience of the world.

>From out the screen of vines and creepers he flung ahead of him a miner's pick and shovel and gold-pan. Then he crawled out himself into the open. He was clad in faded overalls and black cotton shirt, with hobnailed brogans on his feet, and on his head a hat whose shapelessness and stains advertised the rough usage of wind and rain and sun and camp-smoke. He stood erect, seeing wide-eyed the secrecy of the scene and sensuously inhaling the warm, sweet breath of the canyon-garden through nostrils that dilated and quivered with delight. His eyes narrowed to laughing slits of blue, his face wreathed itself in joy, and his mouth curled in a smile as he cried aloud:

"Jumping dandelions and happy hollyhocks, but that smells good to me! Talk about your attar o' roses an' cologne factories! They ain't in it!"

He had the habit of soliloquy. His quick-changing facial expressions might tell every thought and mood, but the tongue, perforce, ran hard after, repeating, like a second Boswell.

The man lay down on the lip of the pool and drank long and deep of its water. "Tastes good to me," he murmured, lifting his head and gazing across the pool at the side-hill, while he wiped his mouth with the back of his hand. The side-hill attracted his attention. Still lying on his stomach, he studied the hill formation long and carefully. It was a practised eye that travelled up the slope to the crumbling canyon-wall and back and down again to the edge of the pool. He scrambled to his feet and favored the side-hill with a second survey.

"Looks good to me," he concluded, picking up his pick and shovel and gold-pan.

He crossed the stream below the pool, stepping agilely from stone to stone. Where the sidehill touched the water he dug up a shovelful of dirt and put it into the gold-pan. He squatted down, holding the pan in his two hands, and partly immersing it in the stream. Then he imparted to the pan a deft circular motion that sent the water sluicing in and out through the dirt and gravel. The larger and the lighter particles worked to the surface, and these, by a skilful dipping movement of the pan, he spilled out and over the edge. Occasionally, to expedite matters, he rested the pan and with his fingers raked out the large pebbles and pieces of rock.

The contents of the pan diminished rapidly until only fine dirt and the smallest bits of gravel remained. At this stage he began to work very deliberately and carefully. It was fine washing, and he washed fine and finer, with a keen scrutiny and delicate and fastidious touch. At last the pan seemed empty of everything but water; but with a quick semicircular flirt that sent the water flying over the shallow rim into the stream, he disclosed a layer of black sand on the bottom of the pan. So thin was this layer that it was like a streak of paint. He examined it closely. In the midst of it was a tiny golden speck. He dribbled a little water in over the depressed edge of the pan. With a quick flirt he sent the water sluicing across the bottom, turning the grains of black sand over and over A second tiny golden speck rewarded his effort.

The washing had now become very fine-fine beyond all need of ordinary placer-mining. He worked the black sand, a small portion at a time, up the shallow rim of the pan. Each small portion he examined sharply, so that his eyes saw every grain of it before he allowed it to slide over the edge and away. Jealously, bit by bit, he let the black sand slip away. A golden speck, no larger than a pin-point, appeared on the rim, and by his manipulation of the riveter it returned to the bottom of tile pan. And in such fashion another speck was disclosed, and another. Great was his care of them. Like a shepherd he herded his flock of golden specks so that not one should be lost. At last, of the pan of dirt nothing remained but his golden herd. He counted it, and then, after all his labor, sent it flying out of the pan with one final swirl of water.

But his blue eyes were shining with desire as he rose to his feet. "Seven," he muttered aloud, asserting the sum of the specks for which he had toiled so hard and which he had so wantonly thrown away. "Seven," he repeated, with the emphasis of one trying to impress a number on his memory.

He stood still a long while, surveying the hill-side. In his eyes was a curiosity, new-aroused and burning. There was an exultance about his bearing and a keenness like that of a hunting animal catching the fresh scent of game.

He moved down the stream a few steps and took a second panful of dirt.

Again came the careful washing, the jealous herding of the golden specks, and the wantonness with which he sent them flying into the stream when he had counted their number.

"Five," he muttered, and repeated, "five."

He could not forbear another survey of the hill before filling the pan farther down the stream. His golden herds diminished. " Four, three, two, two, one," were his memory-tabulations as he moved down the stream. When but one speck of gold rewarded his washing, he stopped and built a fire of dry twigs. Into this he thrust the gold-pan and burned it till it was blue-black. He held up the pan and examined it critically. Then he nodded approbation. Against such a color-background he could defy the tiniest yellow speck to elude him.

Still moving down the stream, he panned again. A single speck was his reward. A third pan contained no gold at all. Not satisfied with this, he panned three times again, taking his shovels of dirt within a foot of one another. Each pan proved empty of gold, and the fact, instead of discouraging him, seemed to give him satisfaction. His elation increased with each barren washing, until he arose, exclaiming jubilantly:

"If it ain't the real thing, may God knock off my head with sour apples!"

Returning to where he had started operations, he began to pan up the stream. At first his golden herds increased-increased prodigiously. " Fourteen, eighteen, twenty-one, twenty-six," ran his memory tabulations. Just above the pool he struck his richest pan-thirty-five colors.

"Almost enough to save," he remarked regretfully as he allowed the water to sweep them away.

The sun climbed to the top of the sky. The man worked on. Pan by pan, he went up the stream, the tally of results steadily decreasing.

"It's just booful, the way it peters out," he exulted when a shovelful of dirt contained no more than a single speck of gold. And when no specks at all were found in several pans, he straightened up and favored the hillside with a confident glance. "Ah, ha! Mr. Pocket!" he cried out, as though to an auditor hidden somewhere above him beneath the surface of the slope. "Ah, ha! Mr. Pocket! I'm a-comin', I'm a-comin', an' I'm shorely gwine to get yer! You heah me, Mr. Pocket? I'm gwine to get yer as shore as punkins ain't cauliflowers!"

He turned and flung a measuring glance at the sun poised above him in the azure of the cloudless sky. Then he went down the canyon, following the line of shovel-holes he had made in filling the pans. He crossed the stream below the pool and disappeared through the green screen. There was little opportunity for the spirit of the place to return with its quietude and repose, for the man's voice, raised in ragtime song, still dominated the canyon with possession.

After a time, with a greater clashing of steel-shod feet on rock, he returned. The green screen was tremendously agitated. It surged back and forth in the throes of a struggle. There was a loud grating and clanging of metal. The man's voice leaped to a higher pitch and was sharp with imperativeness. A large body plunged and panted. There was a snapping and ripping and rending, and amid a shower of falling leaves a horse burst through the screen. On its back was a pack, and from this trailed broken vines and torn creepers. The animal gazed with astonished eyes at the scene into which it had been precipitated, then dropped its head to the grass and began contentedly to graze. A second horse scrambled into view, slipping once on the mossy rocks and regaining equilibrium when its hoofs sank into the yielding surface of the meadow. It was riderless, though on its back was a high-horned Mexican saddle, scarred and discolored by long usage.

The man brought up the rear. He threw off pack and saddle, with an eye to camp location, and gave the animals their freedom to graze. He unpacked his food and got out frying-pan and coffee-pot. He gathered an armful of dry wood, and with a few stones made a place for his fire.

"My!" he said, "but I've got an appetite. I could scoff iron-filings an' horseshoe nails an' thank you kindly, ma'am, for a second helpin'."

He straightened up, and, while he reached for matches in the pocket of his overalls, his eyes travelled across the pool to the side-hill. His fingers had clutched the match-box, but they relaxed their hold and the hand came out empty. The man wavered perceptibly. He looked at his preparations for cooking and he looked at the hill.

"Guess I'll take another whack at her," he concluded, starting to cross the stream.

"They ain't no sense in it, I know," he mumbled apologetically. "But keepin' grub back an hour ain't goin' to hurt none, I reckon."

A few feet back from his first line of test-pans he started a second line. The sun dropped down the western sky, the shadows lengthened, but the man worked on. He began a third line of test-pans. He was cross-cutting the hillside, line by line, as he ascended. The centre of each line produced the richest pans, while the ends came where no colors showed in the pan. And as he ascended the hillside the lines grew perceptibly shorter. The regularity with which their length diminished served to indicate that somewhere up the slope the last line would be so short as to have scarcely length at all, and that beyond could come only a point. The design was growing into an inverted "V." The converging sides of this "V" marked the boundaries of the gold-bearing dirt.

The apex of the "V" was evidently the man's goal. Often he ran his eye along the converging sides and on up the hill, trying to divine the apex, the point where the gold-bearing dirt must cease. Here resided "Mr. Pocket"-for so the man familiarly addressed the imaginary point above him on the slope, crying out:

"Come down out o' that, Mr. Pocket! Be right smart an' agreeable, an' come down!"

"All right," he would add later, in a voice resigned to determination. "All right, Mr. Pocket. It's plain to me I got to come right up an' snatch you out bald-headed. An' I'll do it! I'll do it!" he would threaten still later.

Each pan he carried down to the water to wash, and as he went higher up the hill the pans grew richer, until he began to save the gold in an empty baking-powder can which he carried carelessly in his hip-pocket. So engrossed was he in his toil that he did not notice the long twilight of oncoming night. It was not until he tried vainly to see the gold colors in the bottom of the pan that he realized the passage of time. He straightened up abruptly. An expression of whimsical wonderment and awe overspread his face as he drawled:

"Gosh darn my buttons! if I didn't plumb forget dinner!"

He stumbled across the stream in the darkness and lighted his long-delayed fire. Flapjacks and bacon and warmed-over beans constituted his supper. Then he smoked a pipe by the smouldering coals, listening to the night noises and watching the moonlight stream through the canyon. After that he unrolled his bed, took off his heavy shoes, and pulled the blankets up to his chin. His face showed white in the moonlight, like the face of a corpse. But it was a corpse that knew its resurrection, for the man rose suddenly on one elbow and gazed across at his hillside.

"Good night, Mr. Pocket," he called sleepily. "Good night."

He slept through the early gray of morning until the direct rays of the sun smote his closed eyelids, when he awoke with a start and looked about him until he had established the continuity of his existence and identified his present self with the days previously lived.

To dress, he had merely to buckle on his shoes. He glanced at his fireplace and at his hillside, wavered, but fought down the temptation and started the fire.

"Keep yer shirt on, Bill; keep yer shirt on," he admonished himself. "What's the good of rushin'? No use in gettin' all het up an' sweaty. Mr. Pocket'll wait for you. He ain't a-runnin' away before you can get yer breakfast. Now, what you want, Bill, is something fresh in yer bill o' fare. So it's up to you to go an' get it."

He cut a short pole at the water's edge and drew from one of his pockets a bit of line and a draggled fly that had once been a royal coachman.

"Mebbe they'll bite in the early morning," he muttered, as he made his first cast into the pool. And a moment later he was gleefully crying: "What'd I tell you, eh? What'd I tell you?"

He had no reel, nor any inclination to waste time, and by main strength, and swiftly, he drew out of the water a flashing ten-inch trout. Three more, caught in rapid succession, furnished his breakfast. When he came to the stepping-stones on his way to his hillside, he was struck by a sudden thought, and paused.

"I'd just better take a hike down-stream a ways," he said. "There's no tellin' what cuss may be snoopin' around."

But he crossed over on the stones, and with a "I really oughter take that hike," the need of the precaution passed out of his mind and he fell to work. .

At nightfall he straightened up. The small of his back was stiff from stooping toil, and as he put his hand behind him to soothe the protesting muscles, he said:

"Now what d'ye think of that, by damn? I clean forgot my dinner again! If I don't watch out, I'll sure be degeneratin' into a two-meal-a-day crank."

"Pockets is the damnedest things I ever see for makin' a man absent-minded," he communed that night, as he crawled into his blankets. Nor did he forget to call up the hillside, "Good night, Mr. Pocket! Good night!"

Rising with the sun, and snatching a hasty breakfast, he was early at work. A fever seemed to be growing in him, nor did the increasing richness of the test-pans allay this fever. There was a flush in his cheek other than that made by the heat of the sun, and he was oblivious to fatigue and the passage of time. When he filled a pan with dirt, he ran down the hill to wash it; nor could he forbear running up the hill again, panting and stumbling profanely, to refill the pan.

He was now a hundred yards from the water, and the inverted "V" was assuming definite proportions. The width of the pay-dirt steadily decreased, and the man extended in his mind's eye the sides of the "V" to their meeting-place far up the hill. This was his goal, the apex of the "V," and he panned many times to locate it.

"Just about two yards above that manzanita bush an' a yard to the right," he finally concluded.

Then the temptation seized him. " s plain as the nose on your face," he said, as he abandoned his laborious cross-cutting and climbed to the indicated apex. He filled a pan and carried it down the hill to wash. It contained no trace of gold. He dug deep, and he dug shallow, filling and washing a dozen pans, and was unrewarded even by the tiniest golden speck. He was enraged at having yielded to the temptation, and cursed himself blasphemously and pridelessly. Then he went down the hill and took up the cross-cutting.

"Slow an' certain, Bill; slow an' certain," he crooned. "Short-cuts to fortune ain't in your line, an' it's about time you know it. Get wise, Bill; get wise. Slow an' certain's the only hand you can play; so go to it, an' keep to it, too."

As the cross-cuts decreased, showing that the sides of

the "V" were converging, the depth of the " V " increased. The gold-trace was dipping into the hill. It was only at thirty inches beneath the surface that he could get colors in his pan. The dirt he found at twenty-five inches from the surface, and at thirty-five inches, yielded barren pans. At the base of the "V," by the water's edge, he had found the gold colors at the grass roots. The higher he went up the hill, the deeper the gold dipped.

To dig a hole three feet deep in order to get one test-pan was a task of no mean magnitude; while between the man and the apex intervened an untold number of such holes to be. "An' there's no tellin' how much deeper it'll pitch," he sighed, in a moment's pause, while his fingers soothed his aching back.

Feverish with desire, with aching back and stiffening muscles, with pick and shovel gouging and mauling the soft brown earth, the man toiled up the hill. Before him was the smooth slope, spangled with flowers and made sweet with their breath. Behind him was devastation. It looked like some terrible eruption breaking out on the smooth skin of the hill. His slow progress was like that of a slug, befouling beauty with a monstrous trail.

Though the dipping gold-trace increased the man's work, he found consolation in the increasing richness of the pans. Twenty cents, thirty cents, fifty cents, sixty cents, were the values of the gold found in the pans, and at night-fall he washed his banner pan, which gave him a dollar's worth of gold-dust from a shovelful of dirt.

"I'll just bet it's my luck to have some inquisitive cuss come buttin' in here on my pasture," he mumbled sleepily that night as he pulled the blankets up to his chin.

Suddenly he sat upright. "Bill!" he called sharply. "Now, listen to me, Bill; d'ye hear! It's up to you, to-morrow mornin', to mosey round an' see what you can see. Understand? Tomorrow morning, an' don't you forget it!"

He yawned and glanced across at his side-hill. "Good night, Mr. Pocket," he called.

In the morning he stole a march on the sun, for he had finished breakfast when its first rays caught him, and he was climbing the wall of the canyon where it crumbled away and gave footing. From the outlook at the top he found himself in the midst of loneliness. As far as he could see, chain after chain of mountains heaved themselves into his vision. To the east his eyes, leaping the miles between range and range and between many ranges, brought up at last against the white-peaked Sierras-the main crest, where the backbone of the Western world reared itself against the sky. To the north and south he could see more distinctly the cross-systems that broke through the main trend of the sea of mountains. To the west the ranges fell away, one behind the other, diminishing and fading into the gentle foothills that, in turn, descended into the great valley which he could not see.

And in all that mighty sweep of earth he saw no sign of man nor of the handiwork of man-save only the torn bosom of the hillside at his feet. The man looked long and carefully. Once, far down his own canyon, he thought he saw in the air a faint hint of smoke. He looked again and decided that it was the purple haze of the hills made dark by a convolution of the canyon wall at its back.

"Hey, you, Mr. Pocket!" he called down into the canyon. "Stand out from under! I'm a-comin', Mr. Pocket! I'm a-comin'!"

The heavy brogans on the man's feet made him appear clumsy-footed, but he swung down from the giddy height as lightly and airily as a mountain goat. A rock, turning under his foot on the edge of the precipice, did not disconcert him. He seemed to know the precise time required for the turn to culminate in disaster, and in the meantime he utilized the false footing itself for the momentary earth-contact necessary to carry him on into safety. Where the earth sloped so steeply that it was impossible to stand for a second upright, the man did not hesitate. His foot pressed the impossible surface for but a fraction of the fatal second and gave him the bound that carried him onward. Again, where even the fraction of a second's footing was out of the question, he would swing his body past by a moment's hand-grip on a jutting knob of rock, a crevice, or a precariously rooted shrub. At last, with a wild leap and yell, he exchanged the face of the wall for an earth-slide and finished the descent in the midst of several tons of sliding earth and gravel.

His first pan of the morning washed out over two dollars in coarse gold. It was from the centre of the "V." To either side the diminution in the values of the pans was swift. His lines of crosscutting holes were growing very short. The converging sides of the inverted "V" were only a few yards apart. Their meeting-point was only a few yards above him. But the pay-streak was dipping deeper and deeper into the earth. By early afternoon he was sinking the test-holes five feet before the pans could show the gold-trace.

For that matter, the gold-trace had become something more than a trace; it was a placer mine in itself, and the man resolved to come back after he had found the pocket and work over the ground. But the increasing richness of the pans began to worry him. By late afternoon the worth of the pans had grown to three and four dollars. The man scratched his head perplexedly and looked a few feet up the hill at the manzanita bush that marked approximately the apex of the "V." He nodded his head and said oracularly:

"It's one o' two things, Bill; one o' two things. Either Mr. Pocket's spilled himself all out an' down the hill, or else Mr. Pocket's that damned rich you maybe won't be able to carry him all away with you. And that'd be hell, wouldn't it, now?" He chuckled at contemplation of so pleasant a dilemma.

Nightfall found him by the edge of the stream his eyes wrestling with the gathering darkness over the washing of a five-dollar pan.

"Wisht I had an electric light to go on working." he said.

He found sleep difficult that night. Many times he composed himself and closed his eyes for slumber to overtake him; but his blood pounded with too strong desire, and as many times his eyes opened and he murmured wearily, "Wisht it was sun-up." Sleep came to him in the end, but his eyes were open with the first paling or the stars, and the gray of dawn caught him with breakfast finished and climbing the hillside in the direction of the secret abiding-place of Mr. Pocket.

The first cross-cut the man made, there was space for only three holes, so narrow had become the pay-streak and so close was he to the fountainhead of the golden stream he had been following for four days.

"Be ca'm, Bill; be calm," he admonished himself, as he broke ground for the final hole where the sides of the "V" had at last come together in a point.

"I've got the almighty cinch on you, Mr. Pocket, an' you can't lose me," he said many times as he sank the hole deeper and deeper.

Four feet, five feet, six feet, he dug his way down into the earth. The digging grew harder. His pick grated on broken rock. He examined the rock. "Rotten quartz," was his conclusion as, with the shovel, he cleared the bottom of the hole of loose dirt. He attacked the crumbling quartz with the pick, bursting the disintegrating rock asunder with every stroke.

He thrust his shovel into the loose mass. His eye caught a gleam of yellow. He dropped the shovel and squatted suddenly on his heels. As a farmer rubs the clinging earth from fresh-dug potatoes, so the man, a piece of rotten quartz held in both hands, rubbed the dirt away.

"Sufferin' Sardanopolis!" he cried. "Lumps an' chunks of it! Lumps an' chunks of it!"

It was only half rock he held in his hand. The other half was virgin gold. He dropped it into his pan and examined another piece. Little yellow was to be seen, but with his strong fingers he crumbled the rotten quartz away till both hands were filled with glowing yellow. He rubbed the dirt away from fragment after fragment, tossing them into the gold-pan. It was a treasure-hole. So much had the quartz rotted away that there was less of it than there was of gold. Now and again he found a piece to which no rock clung-a piece that was all gold. A chunk, where the pick had laid open the heart of the gold, glittered like a handful of yellow jewels, and he cocked his head at it and slowly turned it around and over to observe the rich play of the light upon it.

"Talk about yer Too Much Gold diggin's!" the man snorted contemptuously. "Why, this diggin' 'd make it look like thirty cents. This diggin' is All Gold. An' right here an' now I name this yere canyon 'All Gold Canyon,' b' gosh!"

Still squatting on his heels, he continued examining the fragments and tossing them into the pan. Suddenly there came to him a premonition of danger. It seemed a shadow had fallen upon him. But there was no shadow. His heart had given a great jump up into his throat and was choking him. Then his blood slowly chilled and he felt the sweat of his shirt cold against his flesh.

He did not spring up nor look around. He did not move. He was considering the nature of the premonition he had received, trying to locate the source of the mysterious force that had warned him, striving to sense the imperative presence of the unseen thing that threatened him. There is an aura of things hostile, made manifest by messengers refined for the senses to know; and this aura he felt, but knew not how he felt it. His was the feeling as when a cloud

passes over the sun. It seemed that between him and life
had passed something dark and smothering and menacing;
a gloom, as it were, that swallowed up life and made for
death-his death.

Every force of his being impelled him to spring up and
confront the unseen danger, but his soul dominated the
panic, and he remained squatting on his heels, in his hands a
chunk of gold. He did not dare to look around, but he knew
by now that there was something behind him and above him.
He made believe to be interested in the gold in his hand. He
examined it critically, turned it over and over, and rubbed
the dirt from it. And all the time he knew that something
behind him was looking at the gold over his shoulder.

Still feigning interest in the chunk of gold in his hand,
he listened intently and he heard the breathing of the thing
behind him. His eyes searched the ground in front of him
for a weapon, but they saw only the uprooted gold, worthless to him now in his extremity. There was his pick, a handy
weapon on occasion; but this was not such an occasion. The
man realized his predicament. He was in a narrow hole that
was seven feet deep. His head did not come to the surface
of the ground. He was in a trap.

He remained squatting on his heels. He was quite cool
and collected; but his mind, considering every factor,
showed him only his helplessness. He continued rubbing
the dirt from the quartz fragments and throwing the gold
into the pan. There was nothing else for him to do. Yet he
knew that he would have to rise up, sooner or later, and face
the danger that breathed at his back.

The minutes passed, and with the passage of each minute he knew that by so much he was nearer the time when
he must stand up, or else-and his wet shirt went cold against
his flesh again at the thought-or else he might receive death
as he stooped there over his treasure.

Still he squatted on his heels, rubbing dirt from gold and debating in just what manner he should rise up. He might rise up with a rush and claw his way out of the hole to meet whatever threatened on the even footing above ground. Or he might rise up slowly and carelessly, and feign casually to discover the thing that breathed at his back. His instinct and every fighting fibre of his body favored the mad, clawing rush to the surface. His intellect, and the craft thereof, favored the slow and cautious meeting with the thing that menaced and which he could not see. And while he debated, a loud, crashing noise burst on his ear. At the same instant he received a stunning blow on the left side of the back, and from the point of impact felt a rush of flame through his flesh. He sprang up in the air, but halfway to his feet collapsed. His body crumpled in like a leaf withered in sudden heat, and he came down, his chest across his pan of gold, his face in the dirt and rock, his legs tangled and twisted because of the restricted space at the bottom of the hole. His legs twitched convulsively several times. His body was shaken as with a mighty ague. There was a slow expansion of the lungs, accompanied by a deep sigh. Then the air was slowly, very slowly, exhaled, and his body as slowly flattened itself down into inertness.

Above, revolver in hand, a man was peering down over the edge of the hole. He peered for a long time at the prone and motionless body beneath him. After a while the stranger sat down on the edge of the hole so that he could see into it, and rested the revolver on his knee. Reaching his hand into a pocket, he drew out a wisp of brown paper. Into this he dropped a few crumbs of tobacco. The combination became a cigarette, brown and squat, with the ends turned in. Not once did he take his eyes from the body at the bottom of the hole. He lighted the cigarette and drew its smoke into his lungs with a caressing intake of the breath. He smoked slowly. Once the cigarette went out and he relighted it. And all the while he studied the body beneath him.

In the end he tossed the cigarette stub away and rose to his feet. He moved to the edge of the hole. Spanning it, a hand resting on each edge, and with the revolver still in the right hand, he muscled his body down into the hole. While his feet were yet a yard from the bottom he released his hands and dropped down.

At the instant his feet struck bottom he saw the pocket-miner's arm leap out, and his own legs knew a swift, jerking grip that overthrew him. In the nature of the jump his revolver-hand was above his head. Swiftly as the grip had flashed about his legs, just as swiftly he brought the revolver down. He was still in the air, his fall in process of completion, when he pulled the trigger. The explosion was deafening in the confined space. The smoke filled the hole so that he could see nothing. He struck the bottom on his back, and like a cat's the pocket-miner's body was on top of him. Even as the miner's body passed on top, the stranger crooked in his right arm to fire; and even in that instant the miner, with a quick trust of elbow, struck his wrist. The muzzle was thrown up and the bullet thudded into the dirt of the side of the hole.

The next instant the stranger felt the miner's hand grip his wrist. The struggle was now for the revolver. each man strove to turn it against the other's body. The smoke in the hole was clearing. The stranger, lying on his back, was beginning to see dimly. But suddenly he was blinded by a handful of dirt deliberately flung into his eyes by his antagonist. In that moment of shock his grip on the revolver was broken. In the next moment he felt a smashing darkness descend upon his brain, and in the midst of the darkness even the darkness ceased.

But the pocket-miner fired again and again, until the revolver was empty. Then he tossed it from him and, breathing heavily, sat down on the dead man's legs.

The miner was sobbing and struggling for breath. "Measly skunk!" he panted; "a-campin' on my trail an' lettin' me do the work, an' then shootin' me in the back!"

He was half crying from anger and exhaustion, He peered at the face of the dead man. It was sprinkled with loose dirt and gravel, and it was difficult to distinguish the features.

"Never laid eyes on him before," the miner concluded his scrutiny. "Just a common an' ordinary thief, damn him! An' he shot me in the back! He shot me in the back!"

He opened his shirt and felt himself, front and back, on his left side.

"Went clean through, and no harm done!" he cried jubilantly. "I'll bet he aimed right all right, but he drew the gun over when he pulled the trigger-the cuss! But I fixed 'm! Oh, I fixed 'm!"

His fingers were investigating the bullet-hole in his side, and a shade of regret passed over his face. "It's goin' to be stiffer'n hell," he said. "An' it's up to me to get mended an' get out o' here."

He crawled out of the hole and went down the hill to his camp. Half an hour later he returned, leading his pack-horse. His open shirt disclosed the rude bandages with which he had dressed his wound. He was slow and awkward with his left-hand movements, but that did not prevent his using the arm.

The bight of the pack-rope under the dead man's shoulders enabled him to heave the body out of the hole. Then he set to work gathering up his gold. He worked steadily for several hours, pausing often to rest his stiffening shoulder and to exclaim:

"He shot me in the back, the measly skunk! He shot me in the back!"

When his treasure was guise cleaned up and wrapped securely into a number of blanket-covered parcels, he made an estimate of its value.

"Four hundred pounds, or I'm a Hottentot," he concluded. "Say two hundred in quartz an' dirt-that leaves two hun-

dred pounds of gold. Bill! Wake up! Two hundred pounds
of gold! Forty thousand dollars! An' it's yourn-all yourn!"

He scratched his head delightedly and his fingers blun-
dered into an unfamiliar groove. They quested along it for
several inches. It was a crease through his scalp where the
second bullet had ploughed.

He walked angrily over to the dead man.

"You would, would you?" he bullied. "You would, eh?
Well, I fixed you good an' plenty, an' I'll give you decent
burial, too. That's more'n you'd have done for me."

He dragged the body to the edge of the hole and toppled
it in. It struck the bottom with a dull crash, on its side, the
face twisted up to the light. The miner peered down at it.

"An' you shot me in the back!" he said accusingly.

With pick and shovel he filled the hole. Then he loaded
the gold on his horse. It was too great a load for the animal,
and when he had gained his camp he transferred part of it
to his saddle-horse. Even so, he was compelled to abandon
a portion of his outfit-pick and shovel and gold-pan, extra
food and cooking utensils, and divers odds and ends.

The sun was at the zenith when the man forced the
horses at the screen of vines and creepers. To climb the
huge boulders the animals were compelled to uprear and
struggle blindly through the tangled mass of vegetation.
Once the saddle-horse fell heavily and the man removed
the pack to get the animal on its feet. After it started on
its way again the man thrust his head out from among the
leaves and peered up at the hillside.

"The measly skunk!" he said, and disappeared.

There was a ripping and tearing of vines and boughs. The
trees surged back and forth, marking the passage of the animals through the midst of them. There was a clashing of steel-
shod hoofs on stone, and now and again an oath or a sharp cry
of command. Then the voice of the man was raised in song:-

"Tu'n around an' tu'n yo' face
Untoe them sweet hills of grace
(D' pow'rs of sin yo' am scornin'!).
Look about an, look aroun',
Fling yo' sin-pack on d' groun'
(Yo' will meet wid d' Lord in d' mornin'!). "

The song grew faint and fainter, and through the silence crept back the spirit of the place. The stream once more drowsed and whispered; the hum of the mountain bees rose sleepily. Down through the perfume-weighted air fluttered the snowy fluffs of the cottonwoods. The butterflies drifted in and out among the trees, and over all blazed the quiet sunshine. Only remained the hoof-marks in the meadow and the torn hillside to mark the boisterous trail of the life that had broken the peace of the place and passed on.

ON THE DIVIDE

Willa Carther

D ear Rattlesnake Creek, on the side of a little draw stood Canute's shanty. North, east, south, stretched the level Nebraska plain of long rust-red grass that undulated constantly in the wind. To the west the ground was broken and rough, and a narrow strip of timber wound along the turbid, muddy little stream that had scarcely ambition enough to crawl over its black bottom. If it had not been for the few stunted cottonwoods and elms that grew along its banks, Canute would have shot himself years ago. The Norwegians are a timber-loving people, and if there is even a turtle pond with a few plum bushes around it they seem irresistibly drawn toward it.

As to the shanty itself, Canute had built it without aid of any kind, for when he first squatted along the banks of Rattlesnake Creek there was not a human being within twenty miles. It was built of logs split in halves, the chinks stopped with mud and plaster. The roof was covered with earth and was supported by one gigantic beam curved in the shape of a round arch. It was almost impossible that any tree had ever grown in that shape. The Norwegians used to say that Canute had taken the log across his knee and bent it into the shape he wished. There were two rooms, or rather there was one room with a partition made of ash saplings interwoven and bound together like big straw basket work. In one corner there was a cook stove, rusted and broken. In the other a bed made of unplaned planks and poles. It was fully eight feet long, and upon it was a heap of dark bed clothing. There was a chair and a bench of colossal proportions. There was an ordinary kitchen cupboard with a few cracked dirty dishes in it, and beside it on a tall box a tin wash-basin. Under the bed was a pile of pint flasks, some broken, some whole, all empty. On the wood box lay a pair of shoes of almost incredible dimensions. On the wall hung a saddle, a gun, and some ragged clothing, conspicuous among which was a suit of dark cloth, apparently new, with a paper collar carefully wrapped in a red silk handkerchief and pinned to the sleeve. Over the door hung a wolf and a badger skin, and on the door itself a brace of thirty or forty snake skins whose noisy tails rattled ominously every time it opened. The strangest things in the shanty were the wide window-sills. At first glance they looked as though they had been ruthlessly hacked and mutilated with a hatchet, but on closer inspection all the notches and holes in the wood took form and shape. There seemed to be a series of pictures. They were, in a rough way, artistic, but the figures were heavy and labored, as though they had been cut very slowly and with very awkward instruments. There were men plowing with little horned imps sitting on their shoulders and on their horses' heads. There were men praying with a skull hanging over their heads and little demons behind them mocking their attitudes. There were men fighting with big serpents, and skeletons dancing together. All about these pictures were blooming vines and foliage such as never grew in this world, and coiled among the branches of the vines there was always the scaly body of a serpent, and behind every flower there was a serpent's head. It was a veritable Dance of Death by one who had felt its sting. In the wood box lay some boards, and every inch of them was cut up in the same manner. Sometimes the work was very rude and careless, and looked as though the hand of the workman had trembled. It would sometimes have been hard to distinguish the men from their evil geniuses but for one fact, the men were always grave and were either toiling or praying, while the devils were always smiling and dancing. Several of these boards had been split for kindling and it was evident that the artist did not value his work highly.

It was the first day of winter on the Divide. Canute stumbled into his shanty carrying a basket of cobs, and after filling the stove, sat down on a stool and crouched his seven foot frame over the fire, staring drearily out of the window at the wide gray sky. He knew by heart every individual clump of bunch grass in the miles of red shaggy prairie that stretched before his cabin. He knew it in all the deceitful loveliness of its early summer, in all the bitter barrenness of its autumn. He had seen it smitten by all the plagues of Egypt. He had seen it parched by drought, and sogged by rain, beaten by hail, and swept by fire, and in the grasshopper years he had seen it eaten as bare and clean as bones that the vultures have left. After the great fires he had seen it stretch for miles and miles, black and smoking as the floor of hell.

He rose slowly and crossed the room, dragging his big feet heavily as though they were burdens to him. He looked out of the window into the hog corral and saw the pigs burying themselves in the straw before the shed. The leaden gray clouds were beginning to spill themselves, and the snow-flakes were settling down over the white leprous patches of frozen earth where the hogs had gnawed even the sod away. He shuddered and began to walk, trampling heavily with his ungainly feet. He was the wreck of ten winters on the Divide and he knew what they meant. Men fear the winters of the Divide as a child fears night or as men in the North Seas fear the still dark cold of the polar twilight.

His eyes fell upon his gun, and he took it down from the wall and looked it over. He sat down on the edge of his bed and held the barrel towards his face, letting his forehead rest upon it, and laid his finger on the trigger. He was perfectly calm, there was neither passion nor despair in his face, but the thoughtful look of a man who is considering. Presently he laid down the gun, and reaching into the cupboard, drew out a pint bottle of raw white alcohol. Lifting it to his lips, he drank greedily. He washed his face in the tin basin and combed his rough hair and shaggy blond beard.

Then he stood in uncertainty before the suit of dark clothes that hung on the wall. For the fiftieth time he took them in his hands and tried to summon courage to put them on. He took the paper collar that was pinned to the sleeve of the coat and cautiously slipped it under his rough beard, looking with timid expectancy into the cracked, splashed glass that hung over the bench. With a short laugh he threw it down on the bed, and pulling on his old black hat, he went out, striking off across the level.

It was a physical necessity for him to get away from his cabin once in a while. He had been there for ten years, digging and plowing and sowing, and reaping what little the hail and the hot winds and the frosts left him to reap. Insanity and suicide are very common things on the Divide. They come on like an epidemic in the hot wind season. Those scorching dusty winds that blow up over the bluffs from Kansas seem to dry up the blood in men's veins as they do the sap in the corn leaves. Whenever the yellow scorch creeps down over the tender inside leaves about the ear, then the coroners prepare for active duty; for the oil of the country is burned out and it does not take long for the flame to eat up the wick. It causes no great sensation there when a Dane is found swinging to his own windmill tower, and most of the Poles after they have become too careless and discouraged to shave themselves keep their razors to cut their throats with.

It may be that the next generation on the Divide will be very happy, but the present one came too late in life. It is useless for men that have cut hemlocks among the mountains of Sweden for forty years to try to be happy in a country as flat and gray and as naked as the sea. It is not easy for men that have spent their youths fishing in the Northern seas to be content with following a plow, and men that have served in the Austrian army hate hard work and coarse clothing and the loneliness of the plains, and long for marches and excitement and tavern company and pretty barmaids. After a man has passed his fortieth birthday it is not easy for him to change the habits and conditions of his life. Most men bring with them to the Divide only the dregs of the lives that they have squandered in other lands and among other peoples.

Canute Canuteson was as mad as any of them, but his madness did not take the form of suicide or religion but of alcohol. He had always taken liquor when he wanted it, as all Norwegians do, but after his first year of solitary life he settled down to it steadily. He exhausted whisky after a while, and went to alcohol, because its effects were speedier and surer. He was a big man with a terrible amount of resistant force, and it took a great deal of alcohol even to move him. After nine years of drinking, the quantities he could take would seem fabulous to an ordinary drinking man. He never let it interfere with his work, he generally drank at night and on Sundays. Every night, as soon as his chores were done, he began to drink. While he was able to sit up he would play on his mouth harp or hack away at his window sills with his jack knife. When the liquor went to his head he would lie down on his bed and stare out of the window until he went to sleep. He drank alone and in solitude not for pleasure or good cheer, but to forget the awful loneliness and level of the Divide. Milton made a sad blunder when he put mountains in hell. Mountains postulate faith and aspiration. All mountain peoples are religious. It was the cities of the plains that, because of their utter lack of spirituality and the mad caprice of their vice, were cursed of God.

Alcohol is perfectly consistent in its effects upon man. Drunkenness is merely an exaggeration. A foolish man drunk becomes maudlin; a bloody man, vicious; a coarse man, vulgar. Canute was none of these, but he was morose

and gloomy, and liquor took him through all the hells of
Dante. As he lay on his giant's bed all the horrors of this
world and every other were laid bare to his chilled senses.
He was a man who knew no joy, a man who toiled in silence
and bitterness. The skull and the serpent were always before
him, the symbols of eternal futileness and of eternal hate.

When the first Norwegians near enough to be called
neighbors came, Canute rejoiced, and planned to escape
from his bosom vice. But he was not a social man by nature
and had not the power of drawing out the social side of
other people. His new neighbors rather feared him because
of his great strength and size, his silence and his lowering brows. Perhaps, too, they knew that he was mad, mad
from the eternal treachery of the plains, which every spring
stretch green and rustle with the promises of Eden, showing long grassy lagoons full of clear water and cattle whose
hoofs are stained with wild roses. Before autumn the lagoons are dried up, and the ground is burnt dry and hard
until it blisters and cracks open.

So instead of becoming a friend and neighbor to the
men that settled about him, Canute became a mystery and
a terror. They told awful stories of his size and strength and
of the alcohol he drank. They said that one night, when he
went out to see to his horses just before he went to bed, his
steps were unsteady and the rotten planks of the floor gave
way and threw him behind the feet of a fiery young stallion.
His foot was caught fast in the floor, and the nervous horse
began kicking frantically. When Canute felt the blood
trickling down into his eyes from a scalp wound in his head,
he roused himself from his kingly indifference, and with
the quiet stoical courage of a drunken man leaned forward
and wound his arms about the horse's hind legs and held
them against his breast with crushing embrace. All through
the darkness and cold of the night he lay there, matching

strength against strength. When little Jim Peterson went over the next morning at four o'clock to go with him to the Blue to cut wood, he found him so, and the horse was on its fore knees, trembling and whinnying with fear. This is the story the Norwegians tell of him, and if it is true it is no wonder that they feared and hated this Holder of the Heels of Horses.

One spring there moved to the next "eighty" a family that made a great change in Canute's life. Ole Yensen was too drunk most of the time to be afraid of any one, and his wife Mary was too garrulous to be afraid of any one who listened to her talk, and Lena, their pretty daughter, was not afraid of man nor devil. So it came about that Canute went over to take his alcohol with Ole oftener than he took it alone. After a while the report spread that he was going to marry Yensen's daughter, and the Norwegian girls began to tease Lena about the great bear she was going to keep house for. No one could quite see how the affair had come about, for Canute's tactics of courtship were somewhat peculiar. He apparently never spoke to her at all: he would sit for hours with Mary chattering on one side of him and Ole drinking on the other and watch Lena at her work. She teased him, and threw flour in his face and put vinegar in his coffee, but he took her rough jokes with silent wonder, never even smiling. He took her to church occasionally, but the most watchful and curious people never saw him speak to her. He would sit staring at her while she giggled and flirted with the other men.

Next spring Mary Lee went to town to work in a steam laundry. She came home every Sunday, and always ran across to Yensens to startle Lena with stories of ten cent theatres, firemen's dances, and all the other esthetic delights of metropolitan life. In a few weeks Lena's head was completely turned, and she gave her father no rest until he let her go to town to seek her fortune at the ironing board. From the time she came home on her first visit she began to treat Canute with contempt. She had bought a plush cloak and kid gloves, had her clothes made by the dress-maker, and assumed airs and graces that made the other women of the neighborhood cordially detest her. She generally brought with her a young man from town who waxed his mustache and wore a red necktie, and she did not even introduce him to Canute.

The neighbors teased Canute a good deal until he knocked one of them down. He gave no sign of suffering from her neglect except that he drank more and avoided the other Norwegians more carefully than ever. He lay around in his den and no one knew what he felt or thought, but little Jim Peterson, who had seen him glowering at Lena in church one Sunday when she was there with the town man, said that he would not give an acre of his wheat for Lena's life or the town chap's either; and Jim's wheat was so wondrously worthless that the statement was an exceedingly strong one.

Canute had bought a new suit of clothes that looked as nearly like the town man's as possible. They had cost him half a millet crop; for tailors are not accustomed to fitting giants and they charge for it. He had hung those clothes in his shanty two months ago and had never put them on, partly from fear of ridicule, partly from discouragement, and partly because there was something in his own soul that revolted at the littleness of the device.

Lena was at home just at this time. Work was slack in the laundry and Mary had not been well, so Lena stayed at home, glad enough to get an opportunity to torment Canute once more.

She was washing in the side kitchen, singing loudly as she worked. Mary was on her knees, blacking the stove and scolding violently about the young man who was coming out from town that night. The young man had committed the fatal error of laughing at Mary's ceaseless babble and had never been forgiven.

"He is no good, and you will come to a bad end by running with him! I do not see why a daughter of mine should act so. I do not see why the Lord should visit such a punishment upon me as to give me such a daughter. There are plenty of good men you can marry."

Lena tossed her head and answered curtly, "I don't happen to want to marry any man right away, and so long as Dick dresses nice and has plenty of money to spend, there is no harm in my going with him."

"Money to spend? Yes, and that is all he does with it I'll be bound. You think it very fine now, but you will change your tune when you have been married five years and see your children running naked and your cupboard empty. Did Anne Hermanson come to any good end by marrying a town man?"

"I don't know anything about Anne Hermanson, but I know any of the laundry girls would have Dick quick enough if they could get him."

"Yes, and a nice lot of store clothes huzzies you are too. Now there is Canuteson who has an "eighty" proved up and fifty head of cattle and—"

"And hair that ain't been cut since he was a baby, and a big dirty beard, and he wears overalls on Sundays, and drinks like a pig. Besides he will keep. I can have all the fun I want, and when I am old and ugly like you he can have me and take care of me. The Lord knows there ain't nobody else going to marry him."

Canute drew his hand back from the latch as though it were red hot. He was not the kind of man to make a good eavesdropper, and he wished he had knocked sooner. He pulled himself together and struck the door like a battering ram. Mary jumped and opened it with a screech.

"God! Canute, how you scared us! I thought it was crazy Lou,—he has been tearing around the neighborhood trying to convert folks. I am afraid as death of him. He ought to be sent off, I think. He is just as liable as not to kill us all, or burn the barn, or poison the dogs. He has been worrying even the poor minister to death, and he laid up with the rheumatism, too! Did you notice that he was too sick to preach last Sunday? But don't stand there in the cold,—come in. Yensen is n't here, but he just went over to Sorenson's for the mail; he won't be gone long. Walk right in the other room and sit down."

Canute followed her, looking steadily in front of him and not noticing Lena as he passed her. But Lena's vanity would not allow him to pass unmolested. She took the wet sheet she was wringing out and cracked him across the face with it, and ran giggling to the other side of the room. The blow stung his cheeks and the soapy water flew in his eyes, and he involuntarily began rubbing them with his hands. Lena giggled with delight at his discomfiture, and the wrath in Canute's face grew blacker than ever. A big man humiliated is vastly more undignified than a little one. He forgot the sting of his face in the bitter consciousness that he had made a fool of himself. He stumbled blindly into the living room, knocking his head against the door jamb because he forgot to stoop. He dropped into a chair behind the stove, thrusting his big feet back helplessly on either side of him.

Ole was a long time in coming, and Canute sat there, still and silent, with his hands clenched on his knees, and the skin of his face seemed to have shriveled up into little wrinkles that trembled when he lowered his brows. His life had been one long lethargy of solitude and alcohol, but now he was awakening, and it was as when the dumb stagnant heat of summer breaks out into thunder.

When Ole came staggering in, heavy with liquor, Canute rose at once.

"Yensen," he said quietly, "I have come to see if you will let me marry your daughter today."

"Today!" gasped Ole.

"Yes, I will not wait until tomorrow. I am tired of living alone."

Ole braced his staggering knees against the bedstead, and stammered eloquently: "Do you think I will marry my daughter to a drunkard? a man who drinks raw alcohol? a man who sleeps with rattle snakes? Get out of my house or I will kick you out for your impudence." And Ole began looking anxiously for his feet.

Canute answered not a word, but he put on his hat and went out into the kitchen. He went up to Lena and said without looking at her, "Get your things on and come with me!"

The tone of his voice startled her, and she said angrily, dropping the soap, "Are you drunk?"

"If you do not come with me, I will take you,—you had better come," said Canute quietly.

She lifted a sheet to strike him, but he caught her arm roughly and wrenched the sheet from her. He turned to the wall and took down a hood and shawl that hung there, and began wrapping her up. Lena scratched and fought like a wild thing. Ole stood in the door, cursing, and Mary howled and screeched at the top of her voice. As for Canute, he lifted the girl in his arms and went out of the house. She kicked and struggled, but the helpless wailing of Mary and Ole soon died away in the distance, and her face was held down tightly on Canute's shoulder so that she could not see whither he was taking her. She was conscious only of the north wind whistling in her ears, and of rapid steady motion and of a great breast that heaved beneath her in quick, irregular breaths. The harder she struggled the tighter those iron arms that had held the heels of horses crushed about her, until she felt as if they would crush the breath from her, and lay still with fear. Canute was striding across the level fields at a pace at which man never went before, drawing the stinging north wind into his lungs in great gulps. He walked with his eyes half closed and looking straight in front of him, only lowering them when he bent his head to blow away the snowflakes that settled on her hair. So it was that Canute took her to his home, even as his bearded barbarian ancestors took the fair frivolous women of the South in their hairy arms and bore them down to their war ships. For ever and anon the soul becomes weary of the conventions that are not of it, and with a single stroke shatters the civilized lies with which it is unable to cope, and the strong arm reaches out and takes by force what it cannot win by cunning.

When Canute reached his shanty he placed the girl upon a chair, where she sat sobbing. He stayed only a few minutes. He filled the stove with wood and lit the lamp, drank a huge swallow of alcohol and put the bottle in his pocket. He paused a moment, staring heavily at the weeping girl, then he went off and locked the door and disappeared in the gathering gloom of the night.

Wrapped in flannels and soaked with turpentine, the little Norwegian preacher sat reading his Bible, when he heard a thundering knock at his door, and Canute entered, covered with snow and with his beard frozen fast to his coat.

"Come in, Canute, you must be frozen," said the little man, shoving a chair towards his visitor.

Canute remained standing with his hat on and said quietly, "I want you to come over to my house tonight to marry me to Lena Yensen."

"Have you got a license, Canute?"

"No, I don't want a license. I want to be married."

"But I can't marry you without a license, man. It would not be legal."

A dangerous light came in the big Norwegian's eye. "I want you to come over to my house to marry me to Lena Yensen."

"No, I can't, it would kill an ox to go out in a storm like this, and my rheumatism is bad tonight."

"Then if you will not go I must take you," said Canute with a sigh.

He took down the preacher's bearskin coat and bade him put it on while he hitched up his buggy. He went out and closed the door softly after him. Presently he returned and found the frightened minister crouching before the fire with his coat lying beside him. Canute helped him put it on and gently wrapped his head in his big muffler. Then he picked him up and carried him out and placed him in his buggy. As he tucked the buffalo robes around him he said: "Your horse is old, he might flounder or lose his way in this storm. I will lead him."

The minister took the reins feebly in his hands and sat shivering with the cold. Sometimes when there was a lull in the wind, he could see the horse struggling through the snow with the man plodding steadily beside him. Again the blowing snow would hide them from him altogether. He had no idea where they were or what direction they were going. He felt as though he were being whirled away in the heart of the storm, and he said all the prayers he knew. But at last the long four miles were over, and Canute set him down in the snow while he unlocked the door. He saw the bride sitting by the fire with her eyes red and swollen as though she had been weeping. Canute placed a huge chair for him, and said roughly,—

"Warm yourself."

Lena began to cry and moan afresh, begging the minister to take her home. He looked helplessly at Canute. Canute said simply,—

"If you are warm now, you can marry us."

"My daughter, do you take this step of your own free will?" asked the minister in a trembling voice.

"No sir, I don't, and it is disgraceful he should force me into it! I won't marry him."

"Then, Canute, I cannot marry you," said the minister, standing as straight as his rheumatic limbs would let him.

"Are you ready to marry us now, sir?" said Canute, laying one iron hand on his stooped shoulder. The little preacher was a good man, but like most men of weak body he was a coward and had a horror of physical suffering, although he had known so much of it. So with many qualms of conscience he began to repeat the marriage service. Lena sat sullenly in her chair, staring at the fire. Canute stood beside her, listening with his head bent reverently and his hands folded on his breast. When the little man had prayed and said amen, Canute began bundling him up again.

"I will take you home, now," he said as he carried him out and placed him in his buggy, and started off with him through the fury of the storm, floundering among the snow drifts that brought even the giant himself to his knees.

After she was left alone, Lena soon ceased weeping. She was not of a particularly sensitive temperament, and had little pride beyond that of vanity. After the first bitter anger wore itself out, she felt nothing more than a healthy sense of humiliation and defeat. She had no inclination to run away, for she was married now, and in her eyes that was final and all rebellion was useless. She knew nothing about a license, but she knew that a preacher married folks. She consoled herself by thinking that she had always intended to marry Canute some day, any way.

She grew tired of crying and looking into the fire, so she got up and began to look about her. She had heard queer tales about the inside of Canute's shanty, and her curiosity soon got the better of her rage. One of the first things she noticed was the new black suit of clothes hanging on the wall. She was dull, but it did not take a vain woman long to interpret anything so decidedly flattering, and she was pleased in spite of herself. As she looked through the cupboard, the general air of neglect and discomfort made her pity the man who lived there.

"Poor fellow, no wonder he wants to get married to get somebody to wash up his dishes. Batchin's pretty hard on a man."

It is easy to pity when once one's vanity has been tickled. She looked at the window sill and gave a little shudder and wondered if the man were crazy. Then she sat down again and sat a long time wondering what her Dick and Ole would do.

"It is queer Dick didn't come right over after me. He surely came, for he would have left town before the storm began and he might just as well come right on as go back. If he'd hurried he would have gotten here before the preacher came. I suppose he was afraid to come, for he knew Canuteson could"EVEN AS HIS BEARDED BARBARIAN ANCESTORS TOOK THE FAIR FRIVOLOUS WOMEN OF THE SOUTH IN THEIR HAIRY ARMS."pound him to jelly, the coward!" Her eyes flashed angrily.

The weary hours wore on and Lena began to grow horribly lonesome. It was an uncanny night and this was an uncanny place to be in. She could hear the coyotes howling hungrily a little way from the cabin, and more terrible still were all the unknown noises of the storm. She remembered the tales they told of the big log overhead and she was afraid of those snaky things on the win- dow sills. She remembered the man who had been killed in the draw, and she wondered what she would do if she saw crazy Lou's white face glaring into the window. The rattling of the door became unbearable, she thought the latch must be loose and took the lamp to look at it. Then for the first time she saw the ugly brown snake skins whose death rattle sounded every time the wind jarred the door.

"Canute, Canute!" she screamed in terror.

Outside the door she heard a heavy sound as of a big dog getting up and shaking himself. The door opened and Canute stood before her, white as a snow drift.

"What is it?" he asked kindly.

"I am cold," she faltered.

He went out and got an armful of wood and a basket of cobs and filled the stove. Then he went out and lay in the snow before the door. Presently he heard her calling again.

"What is it?" he said, sitting up.

"I 'm so lonesome, I'm afraid to stay in here all alone."

"I will go over and get your mother." And he got up.

"She won't come."

"I'll bring her," said Canute grimly.

"No, no. I don't want her, she will scold all the time."

"Well, I will bring your father."

She spoke again and it seemed as though her mouth was close up to the key-hole. She spoke lower than he had ever heard her speak before, so low that he had to put his ear up to the lock to hear her.

"I don't want him either, Canute,—I 'd rather have you."

For a moment she heard no noise at all, then something like a groan. With a cry of fear she opened the door, and saw Canute stretched in the snow at her feet, his face in his hands, sobbing on the door step.

THE BRIDE COMES TO
YELLOW SKY

Stephen Crane

I

The great Pullman was whirling onward with such dignity of motion that a glance from the window seemed simply to prove that the plains of Texas were pouring eastward. Vast flats of green grass, dull-hued spaces of mesquite and cactus, little groups of frame houses, woods of light and tender trees, all were sweeping into the east, sweeping over the horizon, a precipice.

A newly married pair had boarded this coach at San Antonio. The man's face was reddened from many days in the wind and sun, and a direct result of his new black clothes was that his brick-colored hands were constantly performing in a most conscious fashion. From time to time he looked down respectfully at his attire. He sat with a hand on each knee, like a man waiting in a barber's shop. The glances he devoted to other passengers were furtive and shy.

The bride was not pretty, nor was she very young. She wore a dress of blue cashmere, with small reservations of velvet here and there and with steel buttons abounding. She continually twisted her head to regard her puff sleeves, very stiff, straight, and high. They embarrassed her. It was quite apparent that she had cooked, and that she expected to cook, dutifully. The blushes caused by the careless scrutiny of some passengers as she had entered the car were strange to see upon this plain, under-class countenance, which was drawn in placid, almost emotionless lines.

They were evidently very happy. "Ever been in a parlor-car before?" he asked, smiling with delight.

"No," she answered, "I never was. It's fine, ain't it?"

"Great! And then after a while we'll go forward to the diner and get a big layout. Finest meal in the world. Charge a dollar."

"Oh, do they?" cried the bride. "Charge a dollar? Why, that's too much - for us - ain't it, Jack?"

"Not this trip, anyhow," he answered bravely. "We're going to go the whole thing."

Later, he explained to her about the trains. «You see, it›s a thousand miles from one end of Texas to the other, and this train runs right across it and never stops but four times.» He had the pride of an owner. He pointed out to her the dazzling fittings of the coach, and in truth her eyes opened wider as she contemplated the sea-green figured velvet, the shining brass, silver, and glass, the wood that gleamed as darkly brilliant as the surface of a pool of oil. At one end a bronze figure sturdily held a support for a separated chamber, and at convenient places on the ceiling were frescoes in olive and silver.

To the minds of the pair, their surroundings reflected the glory of their marriage that morning in San Antonio. This was the environment of their new estate, and the man's face in particular beamed with an elation that made him appear ridiculous to the negro porter. This individual at times surveyed them from afar with an amused and superior grin. On other occasions he bullied them with skill in ways that did not make it exactly plain to them that they were being bullied. He subtly used all the manners of the most unconquerable kind of snobbery. He oppressed them, but of this oppression they had small knowledge, and they speedily forgot that infrequently a number of travelers covered them with stares of derisive enjoyment. Historically there was supposed to be something infinitely humorous in their situation.

"We are due in Yellow Sky at 3:42," he said, looking tenderly into her eyes.

"Oh, are we?" she said, as if she had not been aware of it. To evince surprise at her husband's statement was part of her wifely amiability. She took from a pocket a little silver watch, and as she held it before her and stared at it with a frown of attention, the new husband's face shone.

"I bought it in San Anton' from a friend of mine," he told her gleefully.

"It's seventeen minutes past twelve," she said, looking up at him with a kind of shy and clumsy coquetry. A passenger, noting this play, grew excessively sardonic, and winked at himself in one of the numerous mirrors.

At last they went to the dining-car. Two rows of negro waiters, in glowing white suits, surveyed their entrance with the interest and also the equanimity of men who had been forewarned. The pair fell to the lot of a waiter who happened to feel pleasure in steering them through their meal. He viewed them with the manner of a fatherly pilot, his countenance radiant with benevolence. The patronage, entwined with the ordinary deference, was not plain to them. And yet, as they returned to their coach, they showed in their faces a sense of escape.

To the left, miles down a long purple slope, was a little ribbon of mist where moved the keening Rio Grande. The train was approaching it at an angle, and the apex was Yellow Sky. Presently it was apparent that, as the distance from Yellow Sky grew shorter, the husband became commensurately restless. His brick-red hands were more insistent in their prominence. Occasionally he was even rather absent-minded and far-away when the bride leaned forward and addressed him.

As a matter of truth, Jack Potter was beginning to find the shadow of a deed weigh upon him like a leaden slab. He, the town marshal of Yellow Sky, a man known, liked, and feared in his corner, a prominent person, had gone to San Antonio to meet a girl he believed he loved, and there, after the usual prayers, had actually induced her to marry him, without consulting Yellow Sky for any part of the transaction. He was now bringing his bride before an innocent and unsuspecting community.

Of course, people in Yellow Sky married as it pleased them, in accordance with a general custom; but such was Potter's thought of his duty to his friends, or of their idea of his duty, or of an unspoken form which does not control men in these matters, that he felt he was heinous. He had committed an extraordinary crime. Face to face with this girl in San Antonio, and spurred by his sharp impulse, he had gone headlong over all the social hedges. At San Antonio he was like a man hidden in the dark. A knife to sever any friendly duty, any form, was easy to his hand in that remote city. But the hour of Yellow Sky, the hour of daylight, was approaching.

He knew full well that his marriage was an important thing to his town. It could only be exceeded by the burning of the new hotel. His friends could not forgive him. Frequently he had reflected on the advisability of telling them by telegraph, but a new cowardice had been upon him. He feared to do it. And now the train was hurrying him toward a scene of amazement, glee, and reproach. He glanced out of the window at the line of haze swinging slowly in towards the train.

Yellow Sky had a kind of brass band, which played painfully, to the delight of the populace. He laughed without heart as he thought of it. If the citizens could dream of his prospective arrival with his bride, they would parade the band at the station and escort them, amid cheers and laughing congratulations, to his adobe home.

He resolved that he would use all the devices of speed and plains-craft in making the journey from the station to his house. Once within that safe citadel he could issue some sort of a vocal bulletin, and then not go among the citizens until they had time to wear off a little of their enthusiasm.

The bride looked anxiously at him. "What's worrying you, Jack?"

He laughed again. "I'm not worrying, girl. I'm only thinking of Yellow Sky."

She flushed in comprehension.

A sense of mutual guilt invaded their minds and developed a finer tenderness. They looked at each other with eyes softly aglow. But Potter often laughed the same nervous laugh. The flush upon the bride's face seemed quite permanent.

The traitor to the feelings of Yellow Sky narrowly watched the speeding landscape. "We're nearly there," he said.

Presently the porter came and announced the proximity of Potter's home. He held a brush in his hand and, with all his airy superiority gone, he brushed Potter's new clothes as the latter slowly turned this way and that way. Potter fumbled out a coin and gave it to the porter, as he had seen others do. It was a heavy and muscle-bound business, as that of a man shoeing his first horse.

The porter took their bag, and as the train began to slow they moved forward to the hooded platform of the car. Presently the two engines and their long string of coaches rushed into the station of Yellow Sky.

"They have to take water here," said Potter, from a constricted throat and in mournful cadence, as one announcing death. Before the train stopped, his eye had swept the length of the platform, and he was glad and astonished to see there was none upon it but the station-agent, who, with a slightly hurried and anxious air, was walking toward the water-tanks. When the train had halted, the porter alighted first and placed in position a little temporary step.

"Come on, girl," said Potter hoarsely. As he helped her down they each laughed on a false note. He took the bag from the negro, and bade his wife cling to his arm. As they slunk rapidly away, his hang-dog glance perceived that they were unloading the two trunks, and also that the station-agent far ahead near the baggage-car had turned and was running toward him, making gestures. He laughed, and groaned as he laughed, when he noted the first effect of his marital bliss upon Yellow Sky. He gripped his wife's arm firmly to his side, and they fled. Behind them the porter stood chuckling fatuously.

II

The California Express on the Southern Railway was due at Yellow Sky in twenty-one minutes. There were six men at the bar of the "Weary Gentleman" saloon. One was a drummer who talked a great deal and rapidly; three were Texans who did not care to talk at that time; and two were Mexican sheep-herders who did not talk as a general practice in the "Weary Gentleman" saloon. The barkeeper's dog lay on the board walk that crossed in front of the door. His head was on his paws, and he glanced drowsily here and there with the constant vigilance of a dog that is kicked on occasion. Across the sandy street were some vivid green grass plots, so wonderful in appearance amid the sands that burned near them in a blazing sun that they caused a doubt in the mind. They exactly resembled the grass mats used to represent lawns on the stage. At the cooler end of the railway station a man without a coat sat in a tilted chair and smoked his pipe. The fresh-cut bank of the Rio Grande circled near the town, and there could be seen beyond it a great, plum-colored plain of mesquite.

Save for the busy drummer and his companions in the saloon, Yellow Sky was dozing. The new-comer leaned gracefully upon the bar, and recited many tales with the confidence of a bard who has come upon a new field.

" - and at the moment that the old man fell down stairs with the bureau in his arms, the old woman was coming up with two scuttles of coal, and, of course - "

The drummer's tale was interrupted by a young man who suddenly appeared in the open door. He cried: "Scratchy Wilson's drunk, and has turned loose with both hands." The two Mexicans at once set down their glasses and faded out of the rear entrance of the saloon.

The drummer, innocent and jocular, answered: "All right, old man. S'pose he has. Come in and have a drink, anyhow."

But the information had made such an obvious cleft in every skull in the room that the drummer was obliged to see its importance. All had become instantly solemn. "Say," said he, mystified, "what is this?" His three companions made the introductory gesture of eloquent speech, but the young man at the door forestalled them.

"It means, my friend," he answered, as he came into the saloon, "that for the next two hours this town won't be a health resort."

The barkeeper went to the door and locked and barred it. Reaching out of the window, he pulled in heavy wooden shutters and barred them. Immediately a solemn, chapel-like gloom was upon the place. The drummer was looking from one to another.

"But, say," he cried, "what is this, anyhow? You don't mean there is going to be a gun-fight?"

"Don't know whether there'll be a fight or not," answered one man grimly. "But there'll be some shootin' - some good shootin'."

The young man who had warned them waved his hand. "Oh, there'll be a fight fast enough if anyone wants it. Anybody can get a fight out there in the street. There's a fight just waiting."

The drummer seemed to be swayed between the interest of a foreigner and a perception of personal danger.

"What did you say his name was?" he asked.

"Scratchy Wilson," they answered in chorus.

"And will he kill anybody? What are you going to do? Does this happen often? Does he rampage around like this once a week or so? Can he break in that door?"

"No, he can't break down that door," replied the bar-keeper. "He's tried it three times. But when he comes you'd better lay down on the floor, stranger. He's dead sure to shoot at it, and a bullet may come through."

Thereafter the drummer kept a strict eye upon the door. The time had not yet been called for him to hug the floor, but, as a minor precaution, he sidled near to the wall. "Will he kill anybody?" he said again.

The men laughed low and scornfully at the question.

"He's out to shoot, and he's out for trouble. Don't see any good in experimentin' with him."

"But what do you do in a case like this? What do you do?"

A man responded: "Why, he and Jack Potter - "

"But," in chorus, the other men interrupted, "Jack Potter's in San Anton'."

"Well, who is he? What's he got to do with it?"

"Oh, he's the town marshal. He goes out and fights Scratchy when he gets on one of these tears."

"Wow," said the drummer, mopping his brow. "Nice job he's got."

The voices had toned away to mere whisperings. The drummer wished to ask further questions which were born of an increasing anxiety and bewilderment; but when he attempted them, the men merely looked at him in irritation and motioned him to remain silent. A tense waiting hush was upon them. In the deep shadows of the room their eyes shone as they listened for sounds from the street. One man made three gestures at the barkeeper, and the latter, moving like a ghost, handed him a glass and a bottle. The man poured a full glass of whisky, and set down the bottle noiselessly. He gulped the whisky in a swallow, and turned again toward the door in immovable silence. The drummer saw that the barkeeper, without a sound, had taken a Winchester from beneath the bar. Later he saw this individual beckoning to him, so he tiptoed across the room.

«You better come with me back of the bar.»

"No, thanks," said the drummer, perspiring. "I'd rather be where I can make a break for the back door."

Whereupon the man of bottles made a kindly but peremptory gesture. The drummer obeyed it, and finding himself seated on a box with his head below the level of the bar, balm was laid upon his soul at sight of various zinc and copper fittings that bore a resemblance to armor-plate. The barkeeper took a seat comfortably upon an adjacent box.

"You see," he whispered, "this here Scratchy Wilson is a wonder with a gun - a perfect wonder - and when he goes on the war trail, we hunt our holes - naturally. He's about the last one of the old gang that used to hang out along the river here. He's a terror when he's drunk. When he's sober he's all right - kind of simple - wouldn't hurt a fly - nicest fellow in town. But when he's drunk - whoo!"

There were periods of stillness. "I wish Jack Potter was back from San Anton'," said the barkeeper. "He shot Wilson up once - in the leg - and he would sail in and pull out the kinks in this thing."

Presently they heard from a distance the sound of a shot, followed by three wild yowls. It instantly removed a bond from the men in the darkened saloon. There was a shuffling of feet. They looked at each other. "Here he comes," they said.

III

A man in a maroon-colored flannel shirt, which had been purchased for purposes of decoration and made, principally, by some Jewish women on the east side of New York, rounded a corner and walked into the middle of the main street of Yellow Sky. In either hand the man held a long, heavy, blue-black revolver. Often he yelled, and these cries rang through a semblance of a deserted village, shrilly flying over the roofs in a volume that seemed to have no relation to the ordinary vocal strength of a man. It was as if the surrounding stillness formed the arch of a tomb over him. These cries of ferocious challenge rang against walls of silence. And his boots had red tops with gilded imprints, of the kind beloved in winter by little sledding boys on the hillsides of New England.

The man's face flamed in a rage begot of whisky. His eyes, rolling and yet keen for ambush, hunted the still doorways and windows. He walked with the creeping movement of the midnight cat. As it occurred to him, he roared menacing information. The long revolvers in his hands were as easy as straws; they were moved with an electric swiftness. The little fingers of each hand played sometimes in a musician's way. Plain from the low collar of the shirt, the cords of his neck straightened and sank, straightened and sank, as passion moved him. The only sounds were his terrible invitations. The calm adobes preserved their demeanor at the passing of this small thing in the middle of the street.

There was no offer of fight; no offer of fight. The man called to the sky. There were no attractions. He bellowed and fumed and swayed his revolvers here and everywhere.

The dog of the barkeeper of the "Weary Gentleman" saloon had not appreciated the advance of events. He yet lay dozing in front of his master's door. At sight of the dog, the man paused and raised his revolver humorously. At sight of the man, the dog sprang up and walked diagonally away, with a sullen head, and growling. The man yelled, and the dog broke into a gallop. As it was about to enter an alley, there was a loud noise, a whistling, and something spat the ground directly before it. The dog screamed, and, wheeling in terror, galloped headlong in a new direction. Again there was a noise, a whistling, and sand was kicked viciously before it. Fear-stricken, the dog turned and flurried like an animal in a pen. The man stood laughing, his weapons at his hips.

Ultimately the man was attracted by the closed door of the "Weary Gentleman" saloon. He went to it, and hammering with a revolver, demanded drink.

The door remaining imperturbable, he picked a bit of paper from the walk and nailed it to the framework with a knife. He then turned his back contemptuously upon this popular resort, and walking to the opposite side of the street, and spinning there on his heel quickly and lithely, fired at the bit of paper. He missed it by a half inch. He swore at himself, and went away. Later, he comfortably fusilladed the windows of his most intimate friend. The man was playing with this town. It was a toy for him.

But still there was no offer of fight. The name of Jack Potter, his ancient antagonist, entered his mind, and he concluded that it would be a glad thing if he should go to Potter's house and by bombardment induce him to come out and fight. He moved in the direction of his desire, chanting Apache scalp-music.

When he arrived at it, Potter's house presented the same still front as had the other adobes. Taking up a strategic position, the man howled a challenge. But this house regarded him as might a great stone god. It gave no sign. After a decent wait, the man howled further challenges, mingling with them wonderful epithets.

Presently there came the spectacle of a man churning himself into deepest rage over the immobility of a house. He fumed at it as the winter wind attacks a prairie cabin in the North. To the distance there should have gone the sound of a tumult like the fighting of 200 Mexicans. As necessity bade him, he paused for breath or to reload his revolvers.

IV

Potter and his bride walked sheepishly and with speed. Sometimes they laughed together shamefacedly and low.

"Next corner, dear," he said finally.

They put forth the efforts of a pair walking bowed against a strong wind. Potter was about to raise a finger to point the first appearance of the new home when, as they circled the corner, they came face to face with a man in a maroon-colored shirt who was feverishly pushing cartridges into a large revolver. Upon the instant the man dropped his revolver to the ground, and, like lightning, whipped another from its holster. The second weapon was aimed at the bridegroom's chest.

There was silence. Potter's mouth seemed to be merely a grave for his tongue. He exhibited an instinct to at once loosen his arm from the woman's grip, and he dropped the bag to the sand. As for the bride, her face had gone as yellow as old cloth. She was a slave to hideous rites gazing at the apparitional snake.

The two men faced each other at a distance of three paces. He of the revolver smiled with a new and quiet ferocity.

"Tried to sneak up on me," he said. "Tried to sneak up on me!" His eyes grew more baleful. As Potter made a slight movement, the man thrust his revolver venomously forward.

"No, don't you do it, Jack Potter. Don't you move a finger toward a gun just yet. Don't you move an eyelash. The time has come for me to settle with you, and I'm goin' to do it my own way and loaf along with no interferin'. So if you don't want a gun bent on you, just mind what I tell you."

Potter looked at his enemy. "I ain't got a gun on me, Scratchy," he said. "Honest, I ain't." He was stiffening and steadying, but yet somewhere at the back of his mind a vision of the Pullman floated, the sea-green figured velvet, the shining brass, silver, and glass, the wood that gleamed as darkly brilliant as the surface of a pool of oil - all the glory of the marriage, the environment of the new estate. "You know I fight when it comes to fighting, Scratchy Wilson, but I ain't got a gun on me. You'll have to do all the shootin' yourself."

His enemy's face went livid. He stepped forward and lashed his weapon to and fro before Potter's chest. "Don't you tell me you ain't got no gun on you, you whelp. Don't tell me no lie like that. There ain't a man in Texas ever seen you without no gun. Don't take me for no kid." His eyes blazed with light, and his throat worked like a pump.

"I ain't takin' you for no kid," answered Potter. His heels had not moved an inch backward. "I'm takin' you for a damn fool. I tell you I ain't got a gun, and I ain't. If you're goin' to shoot me up, you better begin now. You'll never get a chance like this again."

So much enforced reasoning had told on Wilson's rage. He was calmer. "If you ain't got a gun, why ain't you got a gun?" he sneered. "Been to Sunday-school?"

"I ain't got a gun because I've just come from San Anton' with my wife. I'm married," said Potter. "And if I'd thought there was going to be any galoots like you prowling around when I brought my wife home, I'd had a gun, and don't you forget it."

"Married!" said Scratchy, not at all comprehending.

"Yes, married. I'm married," said Potter distinctly.

"Married?" said Scratchy. Seemingly for the first time he saw the drooping, drowning woman at the other man's side. "No!" he said. He was like a creature allowed a glimpse of another world. He moved a pace backward, and his arm with the revolver dropped to his side. "Is this the lady?" he asked.

"Yes, this is the lady," answered Potter.

There was another period of silence.

"Well," said Wilson at last, slowly, "I s'pose it's all off now."

"It's all off if you say so, Scratchy. You know I didn't make the trouble." Potter lifted his valise.

"Well, I 'low it's off, Jack," said Wilson. He was looking at the ground. "Married!" He was not a student of chivalry; it was merely that in the presence of this foreign condition he was a simple child of the earlier plains. He picked up his starboard revolver, and placing both weapons in their holsters, he went away. His feet made funnel-shaped tracks in the heavy sand.

THE CABALLERO'S WAY

O. Henry

The Cisco Kid had killed six men in more or less fair scrimmages, had murdered twice as many (mostly Mexicans), and had winged a larger number whom he modestly forbore to count. Therefore a woman loved him.

The Kid was twenty-five, looked twenty; and a careful insurance company would have estimated the probable time of his demise at, say, twenty-six. His habitat was anywhere between the Frio and the Rio Grande. He killed for the love of it-because he was quick-tempered- to avoid arrest-for his own amusement-any reason that came to his mind would suffice. He had escaped capture because he could shoot five-sixths of a second sooner than any sheriff or ranger in the service, and because he rode a speckled roan horse that knew every cow-path in the mesquite and pear thickets from San Antonio to Matamoras.

Tonia Perez, the girl who loved the Cisco Kid, was half Carmen, half Madonna, and the rest-oh, yes, a woman who is half Carmen and half Madonna can always be something more-the rest, let us say, was humming-bird. She lived in a grass-roofed jacal near a little Mexican settlement at the Lone Wolf Crossing of the Frio. With her lived a father or grandfather, a lineal Aztec, somewhat less than a thousand years old, who herded a hundred goats and lived in a continuous drunken dream from drinking mescal. Back of the jacal a tremendous forest of bristling pear, twenty feet high at its worst, crowded almost to its door. It was along the bewildering maze of this spinous thicket that the speckled roan would bring the Kid to see his girl. And once, clinging like a lizard to the ridge-pole, high up under the peaked grass roof, he had heard Tonia, with her Madonna face and Carmen beauty and humming-bird soul, parley with the sheriff's posse, denying knowledge of her man in her soft melange of Spanish and English.

One day the adjutant-general of the State, who is, ex offico, commander of the ranger forces, wrote some sarcastic lines to Captain Duval of Company X, stationed at Laredo, relative to the serene and undisturbed existence led by murderers and desperadoes in the said captain's territory.

The captain turned the colour of brick dust under his tan, and forwarded the letter, after adding a few comments, per ranger Private Bill Adamson, to ranger Lieutenant Sandridge, camped at a water hole on the Nueces with a squad of five men in preservation of law and order.

Lieutenant Sandridge turned a beautiful couleur de rose through his ordinary strawberry complexion, tucked the letter in his hip pocket, and chewed off the ends of his gamboge moustache.

The next morning he saddled his horse and rode alone to the Mexican settlement at the Lone Wolf Crossing of the Frio, twenty miles away.

Six feet two, blond as a Viking, quiet as a deacon, dangerous as a machine gun, Sandridge moved among the Jacales, patiently seeking news of the Cisco Kid.

Far more than the law, the Mexicans dreaded the cold and certain vengeance of the lone rider that the ranger sought. It had been one of the Kid's pastimes to shoot Mexicans "to see them kick": if he demanded from them moribund Terpsichorean feats, simply that he might be entertained, what terrible and extreme penalties would be certain to follow should they anger him! One and all they lounged with upturned palms and shrugging shoulders, filling the air with "quien sabes" and denials of the Kid's acquaintance.

But there was a man named Fink who kept a store at the Crossing-a man of many nationalities, tongues, interests, and ways of thinking.

"No use to ask them Mexicans," he said to Sandridge. "They're afraid to tell. This hombre they call the Kid-Goodall is his name, ain't it?-he's been in my store once or twice. I have an idea you might run across him at-but I guess I don't keer to say, myself. I'm two seconds later in pulling a gun than I used to be, and the difference is worth thinking about. But this Kid's got a half-Mexican girl at the Crossing that he comes to see. She lives in that jacal a hundred yards down the arroyo at the edge of the pear. Maybe she-no, I don't suppose she would, but that jacal would be a good place to watch, anyway."

Sandridge rode down to the jacal of Perez. The sun was low, and the broad shade of the great pear thicket already covered the grass- thatched hut. The goats were enclosed for the night in a brush corral near by. A few kids walked the top of it, nibbling the chaparral leaves. The old Mexican lay upon a blanket on the grass, already in a stupor from his mescal, and dreaming, perhaps, of the nights when he and Pizarro touched glasses to their New World fortunes-so old his wrinkled face seemed to proclaim him to be. And in the door of the jacal stood Tonia. And Lieutenant Sandridge sat in his saddle staring at her like a gannet agape at a sailorman.

The Cisco Kid was a vain person, as all eminent and successful assassins are, and his bosom would have been ruffled had he known that at a simple exchange of glances two persons, in whose minds he had been looming large, suddenly abandoned (at least for the time) all thought of him.

Never before had Tonia seen such a man as this. He seemed to be made of sunshine and blood-red tissue and clear weather. He seemed to illuminate the shadow of the pear when he smiled, as though the sun were rising again. The men she had known had been small and dark. Even the Kid, in spite of his achievements, was a stripling no larger than herself, with black, straight hair and a cold, marble face that chilled the noonday.

As for Tonia, though she sends description to the poorhouse, let her make a millionaire of your fancy. Her blueblack hair, smoothly divided in the middle and bound close to her head, and her large eyes full of the Latin melancholy, gave her the Madonna touch. Her motions and air spoke of the concealed fire and the desire to charm that she had inherited from the gitanas of the Basque province. As for the humming-bird part of her, that dwelt in her heart; you could not perceive it unless her bright red skirt and dark blue blouse gave you a symbolic hint of the vagarious bird.

The newly lighted sun-god asked for a drink of water. Tonia brought it from the red jar hanging under the brush shelter. Sandridge considered it necessary to dismount so as to lessen the trouble of her ministrations.

I play no spy; nor do I assume to master the thoughts of any human heart; but I assert, by the chronicler's right, that before a quarter of an hour had sped, Sandridge was teaching her how to plaint a six-strand rawhide stake-rope, and Tonia had explained to him that were it not for her little English book that the peripatetic padre had given her and the little crippled chivo, that she fed from a bottle, she would be very, very lonely indeed.

Which leads to a suspicion that the Kid's fences needed repairing, and that the adjutant-general's sarcasm had fallen upon unproductive soil.

In his camp by the water hole Lieutenant Sandridge announced and reiterated his intention of either causing the Cisco Kid to nibble the black loam of the Frio country prairies or of haling him before a judge and jury. That sounded business-like. Twice a week he rode over to the Lone Wolf Crossing of the Frio, and directed Tonia's slim, slightly lemon-tinted fingers among the intricacies of the slowly growing lariata. A six-strand plait is hard to learn and easy to teach.

The ranger knew that he might find the Kid there at any visit. He kept his armament ready, and had a frequent eye for the pear thicket at the rear of the jacal. Thus he might bring down the kite and the humming-bird with one stone.

While the sunny-haired ornithologist was pursuing his studies the Cisco Kid was also attending to his professional duties. He moodily shot up a saloon in a small cow village on Quintana Creek, killed the town marshal (plugging him neatly in the centre of his tin badge), and then rode away, morose and unsatisfied. No true artist is uplifted by shooting an aged man carrying an old-style .38 bulldog.

On his way the Kid suddenly experienced the yearning that all men feel when wrong-doing loses its keen edge of delight. He yearned for the woman he loved to reassure him that she was his in spite of it. He wanted her to call his bloodthirstiness bravery and his cruelty devotion. He wanted Tonia to bring him water from the red jar under the brush shelter, and tell him how the chivo was thriving on the bottle.

The Kid turned the speckled roan's head up the ten-mile pear flat that stretches along the Arroyo Hondo until it ends at the Lone Wolf Crossing of the Frio. The roan whickered; for he had a sense of locality and direction equal to that of a belt-line street-car horse; and he knew he would soon be nibbling the rich mesquite grass at the end of a forty-foot stake-rope while Ulysses rested his head in Circe's straw-roofed hut.

More weird and lonesome than the journey of an Amazonian explorer is the ride of one through a Texas pear flat. With dismal monotony and startling variety the uncanny and multiform shapes of the cacti lift their twisted trunks, and fat, bristly hands to encumber the way. The demon plant, appearing to live without soil or rain, seems to taunt the parched traveller with its lush grey greenness. It warps itself a thousand times about what look to be open and inviting paths, only to lure the rider into blind and impassable spine-defended "bottoms of the bag," leaving him to retreat, if he can, with the points of the compass whirling in his head.

To be lost in the pear is to die almost the death of the thief on the cross, pierced by nails and with grotesque shapes of all the fiends hovering about.

But it was not so with the Kid and his mount. Winding, twisting, circling, tracing the most fantastic and bewildering trail ever picked out, the good roan lessened the distance to the Lone Wolf Crossing with every coil and turn that he made.

While they fared the Kid sang. He knew but one tune and sang it, as he knew but one code and lived it, and but one girl and loved her. He was a single-minded man of conventional ideas. He had a voice like a coyote with bronchitis, but whenever he chose to sing his song he sang it. It was a conventional song of the camps and trail, running at its beginning as near as may be to these words:

Don't you monkey with my Lulu girl
Or I'll tell you what I'll do-

and so on. The roan was inured to it, and did not mind.

But even the poorest singer will, after a certain time, gain his own consent to refrain from contributing to the world's noises. So the Kid, by the time he was within a mile or two of Tonia's jacal, had reluctantly allowed his song to die away-not because his vocal performance had become less charming to his own ears, but because his laryngeal muscles were aweary.

As though he were in a circus ring the speckled roan wheeled and danced through the labyrinth of pear until at length his rider knew by certain landmarks that the Lone Wolf Crossing was close at hand. Then, where the pear was thinner, he caught sight of the grass roof of the jacal and the hackberry tree on the edge of the arroyo. A few yards farther the Kid stopped the roan and gazed intently through the prickly openings. Then he dismounted, dropped the roan's reins, and proceeded on foot, stooping and silent, like an Indian. The roan, knowing his part, stood still, making no sound.

The Kid crept noiselessly to the very edge of the pear thicket and reconnoitred between the leaves of a clump of cactus.

Ten yards from his hiding-place, in the shade of the jacal, sat his Tonia calmly plaiting a rawhide lariat. So far she might surely escape condemnation; women have been known, from time to time, to engage in more mischievous occupations. But if all must be told, there is to be added that her head reposed against the broad and comfortable chest of a tall red-and-yellow man, and that his arm was about her, guiding her nimble fingers that required so many lessons at the intricate six- strand plait.

Sandridge glanced quickly at the dark mass of pear when he heard a slight squeaking sound that was not altogether unfamiliar. A gun- scabbard will make that sound when one grasps the handle of a six- shooter suddenly. But the sound was not repeated; and Tonia's fingers needed close attention.

And then, in the shadow of death, they began to talk of their love; and in the still July afternoon every word they uttered reached the ears of the Kid.

"Remember, then," said Tonia, "you must not come again until I send for you. Soon he will be here. A vaquero at the tienda said to-day he saw him on the Guadalupe three days ago. When he is that near he always comes. If he comes and finds you here he will kill you. So, for my sake, you must come no more until I send you the word."

"All right," said the stranger. "And then what?"

"And then," said the girl, "you must bring your men here and kill him. If not, he will kill you."

"He ain't a man to surrender, that's sure," said Sandridge. "It's kill or be killed for the officer that goes up against Mr. Cisco Kid."

"He must die," said the girl. "Otherwise there will not be any peace in the world for thee and me. He has killed many. Let him so die. Bring your men, and give him no chance to escape."

"You used to think right much of him," said Sandridge.

Tonia dropped the lariat, twisted herself around, and curved a lemon- tinted arm over the ranger's shoulder.

"But then," she murmured in liquid Spanish, "I had not beheld thee, thou great, red mountain of a man! And thou art kind and good, as well as strong. Could one choose him, knowing thee? Let him die; for then I will not be filled with fear by day and night lest he hurt thee or me."

"How can I know when he comes?" asked Sandridge.

"When he comes," said Tonia, "he remains two days, sometimes three. Gregorio, the small son of old Luisa, the lavendera, has a swift pony. I will write a letter to thee and send it by him, saying how it will be best to come upon him. By Gregorio will the letter come. And bring many men with thee, and have much care, oh, dear red one, for the rattle-snake is not quicker to strike than is 'El Chivato,' as they call him, to send a ball from his pistola."

"The Kid's handy with his gun, sure enough," admitted Sandridge, "but when I come for him I shall come alone. I'll get him by myself or not at all. The Cap wrote one or two things to me that make me want to do the trick without any help. You let me know when Mr. Kid arrives, and I'll do the rest."

"I will send you the message by the boy Gregorio," said the girl. "I knew you were braver than that small slayer of men who never smiles. How could I ever have thought I cared for him?"

It was time for the ranger to ride back to his camp on the water hole. Before he mounted his horse he raised the slight form of Tonia with one arm high from the earth for a parting salute. The drowsy stillness of the torpid summer air still lay thick upon the dreaming afternoon. The smoke from the fire in the jacal, where the frijoles blubbered in the iron pot, rose straight as a plumb-line above the clay-daubed chimney. No sound or movement disturbed the serenity of the dense pear thicket ten yards away.

When the form of Sandridge had disappeared, loping his big dun down the steep banks of the Frio crossing, the Kid crept back to his own horse, mounted him, and rode back along the tortuous trail he had come.

But not far. He stopped and waited in the silent depths of the pear until half an hour had passed. And then Tonia heard the high, untrue notes of his unmusical singing coming nearer and nearer; and she ran to the edge of the pear to meet him.

The Kid seldom smiled; but he smiled and waved his hat when he saw her. He dismounted, and his girl sprang into his arms. The Kid looked at her fondly. His thick, black hair clung to his head like a wrinkled mat. The meeting brought a slight ripple of some undercurrent of feeling to his smooth, dark face that was usually as motionless as a clay mask.

"How's my girl?" he asked, holding her close.

"Sick of waiting so long for you, dear one," she answered. "My eyes are dim with always gazing into that devil's pincushion through which you come. And I can see into it such a little way, too. But you are here, beloved one, and I will not scold. Que mal muchacho! not to come to see your alma more often. Go in and rest, and let me water your horse and stake him with the long rope. There is cool water in the jar for you."

The Kid kissed her affectionately.

"Not if the court knows itself do I let a lady stake my horse for me," said he. "But if you'll run in, chica, and throw a pot of coffee together while I attend to the caballo, I'll be a good deal obliged."

Besides his marksmanship the Kid had another attribute for which he admired himself greatly. He was muy caballero, as the Mexicans express it, where the ladies were concerned. For them he had always gentle words and consideration. He could not have spoken a harsh word to a woman. He might ruthlessly slay their husbands and brothers, but he could not have laid the weight of a finger in anger upon a woman. Wherefore many of that interesting division of humanity who had come under the spell of his politeness declared their disbelief in the stories circulated about Mr. Kid. One shouldn't believe everything one heard, they said. When confronted by their indignant men folk with proof of the caballero's deeds of infamy, they said maybe he had been driven to it, and that he knew how to treat a lady, anyhow.

Considering this extremely courteous idiosyncrasy of the Kid and the pride he took in it, one can perceive that the solution of the problem that was presented to him by what he saw and heard from his hiding- place in the pear that afternoon (at least as to one of the actors) must have been obscured by difficulties. And yet one could not think of the Kid overlooking little matters of that kind.

At the end of the short twilight they gathered around a supper of frijoles, goat steaks, canned peaches, and coffee, by the light of a lantern in the jacal. Afterward, the ancestor, his flock corralled, smoked a cigarette and became a mummy in a grey blanket. Tonia washed the few dishes while the Kid dried them with the flour-sacking towel. Her eyes shone; she chatted volubly of the inconsequent happenings of her small world since the Kid's last visit; it was as all his other home-comings had been.

Then outside Tonia swung in a grass hammock with her guitar and sang sad canciones de amor.

"Do you love me just the same, old girl?" asked the Kid, hunting for his cigarette papers.

"Always the same, little one," said Tonia, her dark eyes lingering upon him.

"I must go over to Fink's," said the Kid, rising, "for some tobacco. I thought I had another sack in my coat. I'll be back in a quarter of an hour."

"Hasten," said Tonia, "and tell me-how long shall I call you my own this time? Will you be gone again to-morrow, leaving me to grieve, or will you be longer with your Tonia?"

"Oh, I might stay two or three days this trip," said the Kid, yawning. "I've been on the dodge for a month, and I'd like to rest up."

He was gone half an hour for his tobacco. When he returned Tonia was still lying in the hammock.

"It's funny," said the Kid, "how I feel. I feel like there was somebody lying behind every bush and tree waiting to shoot me. I never had mullygrubs like them before. Maybe it's one of them presumptions. I've got half a notion to light out in the morning before day. The Guadalupe country is burning up about that old Dutchman I plugged down there."

"You are not afraid-no one could make my brave little one fear."

"Well, I haven't been usually regarded as a jack-rabbit when it comes to scrapping; but I don't want a posse smoking me out when I'm in your jacal. Somebody might get hurt that oughtn't to."

"Remain with your Tonia; no one will find you here."

The Kid looked keenly into the shadows up and down the arroyo and toward the dim lights of the Mexican village.

"I'll see how it looks later on," was his decision.

At midnight a horseman rode into the rangers' camp, blazing his way by noisy "halloes" to indicate a pacific mission. Sandridge and one or two others turned out to investigate the row. The rider announced himself to be Domingo Sales, from the Lone Wolf Crossing. he bore a letter for Senor Sandridge. Old Luisa, the lavendera, had persuaded him to bring it, he said, her son Gregorio being too ill of a fever to ride.

Sandridge lighted the camp lantern and read the letter. These were its words:

Dear One: He has come. Hardly had you ridden away when he came out of the pear. When he first talked he said he would stay three days or more. Then as it grew later he was like a wolf or a fox, and walked about without rest, looking and listening. Soon he said he must leave before daylight when it is dark and stillest. And then he seemed to suspect that I be not true to him. He looked at me so strange that I am frightened. I swear to him that I love him, his own Tonia. Last of all he said I must prove to him I am true. He thinks that even now men are waiting to kill him as he rides from my house. To escape he says he will dress in my clothes, my red skirt and the blue waist I wear and the brown mantilla over the head, and thus ride away. But before that he says that I must put on his clothes, his pantalones and camisa and hat, and ride away on his horse from the jacal as far as the big road beyond the crossing and back again. This before he goes, so he can tell if I am true and if men are hidden to shoot him. It is a terrible thing. An hour before daybreak this is to be. Come, my dear one, and kill this man and take me for your Tonia. Do not try to take hold of him alive, but kill him quickly. Knowing all, you should do that. You must come long before the time and hide yourself in the little shed near the jacal where the wagon and saddles are kept. It is dark in there. He will wear my red skirt and blue waist and brown mantilla. I send you a hundred kisses. Come surely and shoot quickly and straight. Thine Own Tonia.

Sandridge quickly explained to his men the official part of the missive. The rangers protested against his going alone.

"I'll get him easy enough," said the lieutenant. "The girl's got him trapped. And don't even think he'll get the drop on me."

Sandridge saddled his horse and rode to the Lone Wolf Crossing. He tied his big dun in a clump of brush on the arroyo, took his Winchester from its scabbard, and carefully approached the Perez jacal. There was only the half of a high moon drifted over by ragged, milk-white gulf clouds.

The wagon-shed was an excellent place for ambush; and the ranger got inside it safely. In the black shadow of the brush shelter in front of the jacal he could see a horse tied and hear him impatiently pawing the hard-trodden earth.

He waited almost an hour before two figures came out of the jacal. One, in man's clothes, quickly mounted the horse and galloped past the wagon-shed toward the crossing and village. And then the other figure, in skirt, waist, and mantilla over its head, stepped out into the faint moonlight, gazing after the rider. Sandridge thought he would take his chance then before Tonia rode back. He fancied she might not care to see it.

"Throw up your hands," he ordered loudly, stepping out of the wagon- shed with his Winchester at his shoulder.

There was a quick turn of the figure, but no movement to obey, so the ranger pumped in the bullets-one-two-three-and then twice more; for you never could be too sure of bringing down the Cisco Kid. There was no danger of missing at ten paces, even in that half moonlight.

The old ancestor, asleep on his blanket, was awakened by the shots. Listening further, he heard a great cry from some man in mortal distress or anguish, and rose up grumbling at the disturbing ways of moderns.

The tall, red ghost of a man burst into the jacal, reaching one hand, shaking like a tule reed, for the lantern hanging on its nail. The other spread a letter on the table.

"Look at this letter, Perez," cried the man. "Who wrote it?"

"Ah, Dios! it is Senor Sandridge," mumbled the old man, approaching. "Pues, senor, that letter was written by 'El

Chivato,' as he is called-by the man of Tonia. They say he is a bad man; I do not know. While Tonia slept he wrote the letter and sent it by this old hand of mine to Domingo Sales to be brought to you. Is there anything wrong in the letter? I am very old; and I did not know. Valgame Dios! it is a very foolish world; and there is nothing in the house to drink- nothing to drink."

Just then all that Sandridge could think of to do was to go outside and throw himself face downward in the dust by the side of his humming-bird, of whom not a feather fluttered. He was not a caballero by instinct, and he could not understand the niceties of revenge.

A mile away the rider who had ridden past the wagon-shed struck up a harsh, untuneful song, the words of which began:

Don't you monkey with my Lulu girl Or I'll tell you what I'll do-

THE GREAT SLAVE

Zane Grey

A voice on the wind whispered to Siena the prophecy of his birth. "A chief is born to save the vanishing tribe of Crows! A hunter to his starving people!" While he listened, at his feet swept swift waters, the rushing, green-white, thundering Athabasca, spirit-forsaken river; and it rumbled his name and murmured his fate. "Siena! Siena! His bride will rise from a wind kiss on the flowers in the moonlight! A new land calls to the last of the Crows! Northward where the wild goose ends its flight Siena will father a great people!"

So Siena, a hunter of the leafy trails, dreamed his dreams; and at sixteen he was the hope of the remnant of a once powerful tribe, a stripling chief, beautiful as a bronzed autumn god, silent, proud, forever listening to voices on the wind.

To Siena the lore of the woodland came as flight comes to the strong-winged wild fowl. The secrets of the forests were his, and of the rocks and rivers.

He knew how to find the nests of the plover, to call the loon, to net the heron, and spear the fish. He understood the language of the whispering pines. Where the deer came down to drink and the caribou browsed on moss and the white rabbit nibbled in the grass and the bear dug in the logs for grubs—all these he learned; and also when the black flies drove the moose into the water and when the honk of the geese meant the approach of the north wind.

He lived in the woods, with his bow, his net, and his spear. The trees were his brothers. The loon laughed for his happiness, the wolf mourned for his sadness. The bold crag above the river, Old Stoneface, heard his step when he climbed there in the twilight. He communed with the stern god of his ancestors and watched the flashing Northern Lights and listened.

From all four corners came his spirit guides with steps of destiny on his trail. On all the four winds breathed voices whispering of his future; loudest of all called the Athabasca, god-forsaken river, murmuring of the bride born of a wind kiss on the flowers in the moonlight.

On all the four winds breathed voices whispering of his future.

It was autumn, with the flame of leaf fading, the haze rolling out of the hollows, the lull yielding to moan of coming wind. All the signs of a severe winter were in the hulls of the nuts, in the fur of the foxes, in the flight of waterfowl. Siena was spearing fish for winter store. None so keen of sight as Siena, so swift of arm; and as he was the hope, so he alone was the provider for the starving tribe. Siena stood to his knees in a brook where it flowed over its gravelly bed into the Athabasca. Poised high was his wooden spear. It glinted downward swift as a shaft of sunlight through the leaves. Then Siena lifted a quivering whitefish and tossed it upon the bank where his mother Ema, with other women of the tribe, sun-dried the fish upon a rock.

Again and again, many times, flashed the spear. The young chief seldom missed his aim. Early frosts on the uplands had driven the fish down to deeper water, and as they came darting over the bright pebbles Siena called them by name.

The oldest squaw could not remember such a run of fish. Ema sang the praises of her son; the other women ceased the hunger chant of the tribe.

Suddenly a hoarse shout pealed out over the waters.

Ema fell in a fright; her companions ran away; Siena leaped upon the bank, clutching his spear. A boat in which were men with white faces drifted down toward him.

"Hal-loa!" again sounded the hoarse cry.

Ema cowered in the grass. Siena saw a waving of white hands; his knees knocked together and he felt himself about to flee. But Siena of the Crows, the savior of a vanishing tribe, must not fly from visible foes.

"Palefaces," he whispered, trembling, yet stood his ground ready to fight for his mother. He remembered stories of an old

Indian who had journeyed far to the south and had crossed the trails of the dreaded white men. There stirred in him vague memories of strange Indian runners telling camp-fire tales of white hunters with weapons of lightning and thunder.

"Naza! Naza!" Siena cast one fleeting glance to the north and a prayer to his god of gods. He believed his spirit would soon be wandering in the shades of the other Indian world.

As the boat beached on the sand Siena saw men lying with pale faces upward to the sky, and voices in an unknown tongue greeted him. The tone was friendly, and he lowered his threatening spear. Then a man came up the bank, his hungry eyes on the pile of fish, and he began to speak haltingly in mingled Cree and Chippewayan language:

"Boy—we're white friends—starving—let us buy fish—trade for fish—we're starving and we have many moons to travel."

"Siena's tribe is poor," replied the lad; "sometimes they starve too. But Siena will divide his fish and wants no trade."

His mother, seeing the white men intended no evil, came out of her fright and complained bitterly to Siena of his liberality. She spoke of the menacing winter, of the frozen streams, the snow-bound forest, the long night of hunger. Siena silenced her and waved the frightened braves and squaws back to their wigwams.

"Siena is young," he said simply; "but he is chief here. If we starve—we starve."

Whereupon he portioned out a half of the fish. The white men built a fire and sat around it feasting like famished wolves around a fallen stag. When they had appeased their hunger they packed the remaining fish in the boat, whistling and singing the while. Then the leader made offer to pay, which Siena refused, though the covetous light in his mother's eyes hurt him sorely.

"Chief," said the leader, "the white man understands; now he offers presents as one chief to another."

Thereupon he proffered bright beads and tinseled trinkets, yards of calico and strips of cloth. Siena accepted with a dignity in marked contrast to the way in which the greedy Ema pounced upon the glittering heap. Next the paleface presented a knife which, drawn from its scabbard, showed a blade that mirrored its brightness in Siena's eyes.

"Chief, your woman complains of a starving tribe," went on the white man. "Are there not many moose and reindeer?"

"Yes. But seldom can Siena creep within range of his arrow."

"A-ha! Siena will starve no more," replied the man, and from the boat he took a long iron tube with a wooden stock.

"What is that?" asked Siena.

"The wonderful shooting stick. Here, boy, watch! See the bark on the camp fire. Watch!"

He raised the stick to his shoulder. Then followed a streak of flame, a puff of smoke, a booming report; and the bark of the camp fire flew into bits.

The children dodged into the wigwams with loud cries, the women ran screaming, Ema dropped in the grass wailing that the end of the world had come, while Siena, unable to move hand or foot, breathed another prayer to Naza of the northland.

The white man laughed and, patting Siena's arm, he said: "No fear." Then he drew Siena away from the bank, and began to explain the meaning and use of the wonderful shooting stick. He reloaded it and fired again and yet again, until Siena understood and was all aflame at the possibilities of such a weapon.

Patiently the white man taught the Indian how to load it, sight, and shoot, and how to clean it with ramrod and buckskin. Next he placed at Siena's feet a keg of powder, a bag of lead bullets, and boxes full of caps. Then he bade Siena farewell, entered the boat with his men and drifted round a bend of the swift Athabasca.

Siena stood alone upon the bank, the wonderful shooting stick in his hands, and the wail of his frightened mother in his ears. He comforted her, telling her the white men were gone, that he was safe, and that the prophecy of his birth had at last begun its fulfillment. He carried the precious ammunition to a safe hiding place in a hollow log near his wigwam and then he plunged into the forest.

Siena bent his course toward the runways of the moose. He walked in a kind of dream, for he both feared and believed. Soon the glimmer of water, splashes and widening ripples, caused him to crawl stealthily through the ferns and grasses to the border of a pond. The familiar hum of flies told him of the location of his quarry. The moose had taken to the water, driven by the swarms of black flies, and were standing neck deep, lifting their muzzles to feed on the drooping poplar branches. Their widespreading antlers, tipped back into the water, made the ripples.

Trembling as never before, Siena sank behind a log. He was within fifty paces of the moose. How often in that very spot had he strung a feathered arrow and shot it vainly! But now he had the white man's weapon, charged with lightning and thunder. Just then the poplars parted above the shore, disclosing a bull in the act of stepping down. He tossed his antlered head at the cloud of humming flies, then stopped, lifting his nose to scent the wind.

"Naza!" whispered Siena in his swelling throat.

He rested the shooting stick on the log and tried to see over the brown barrel. But his eyes were dim. Again he whispered a prayer to Naza. His sight cleared, his shaking arms stilled, and with his soul waiting, hoping, doubting, he aimed and pulled the trigger.

Boom!

High the moose flung his ponderous head, to crash down upon his knees, to roll in the water and churn a bloody foam, and then lie still.

"Siena! Siena!"

Shrill the young chief's exultant yell pealed over the listening waters, piercing the still forest, to ring back in echo from Old Stoneface. It was Siena's triumphant call to his forefathers, watching him from the silence.

The herd of moose plowed out of the pond and crashed into the woods, where, long after they had disappeared, their antlers could be heard cracking the saplings.

When Siena stood over the dead moose his doubts fled; he was indeed god chosen. No longer chief of a starving tribe! Reverently and with immutable promise he raised the shooting stick to the north, toward Naza who had remembered him; and on the south, where dwelt the enemies of his tribe, his dark glance brooded wild and proud and savage.

Eight times the shooting stick boomed out in the stillness and eight moose lay dead in the wet grasses. In the twilight Siena wended his way home and placed eight moose tongues before the whimpering squaws.

"Siena is no longer a boy," he said. "Siena is a hunter. Let his women go bring in the meat."

Then to the rejoicing and feasting and dancing of his tribe he turned a deaf ear, and in the night passed alone under the shadow of Old Stoneface, where he walked with the spirits of his ancestors and believed the voices on the wind.

Before the ice locked the ponds Siena killed a hundred moose and reindeer. Meat and fat and oil and robes changed the world for the Crow tribe.

Fires burned brightly all the long winter; the braves awoke from their stupor and chanted no more; the women sang of the Siena who had come, and prayed for summer wind and moonlight to bring his bride.

Spring went by, summer grew into blazing autumn, and Siena's fame and the wonder of the shooting stick spread through the length and breadth of the land.

Another year passed, then another, and Siena was the great chief of the rejuvenated Crows. He had grown into a warrior's stature, his face had the beauty of the god chosen, his eye the falcon flash of the Sienas of old. Long communion in the shadow of Old Stoneface had added wisdom to his other gifts; and now to his worshiping tribe all that was needed to complete the prophecy of his birth was the coming of the alien bride.

It was another autumn, with the wind whipping the tamaracks and moaning in the pines, and Siena stole along a brown, fern-lined trail. The dry smell of fallen leaves filled his nostrils; he tasted snow in the keen breezes. The flowers were dead, and still no dark-eyed bride sat in his wigwam. Siena sorrowed and strengthened his heart to wait. He saw her flitting in the shadows around him, a wraith with dusky eyes veiled by dusky wind-blown hair, and ever she hovered near him, whispering from every dark pine, from every waving tuft of grass.

To her whispers he replied: "Siena waits."

He wondered of what alien tribe she would come. He hoped not of the unfriendly Chippewayans or the far-distant Blackfeet; surely not of the hostile Crees, life enemies of his tribe, destroyers of its once puissant strength, jealous now of its resurging power.

Other shadows flitted through the forest, spirits that rose silently from the graves over which he trod, and warned him of double steps on his trail, of unseen foes watching him from the dark coverts. His braves had repeated gossip, filterings from stray Indian wanderers, hinting of plots against the risen Siena. To all these he gave no heed, for was not he Siena, god-chosen, and had he not the wonderful shooting stick?

It was the season that he loved, when dim forest and hazy fernland spoke most impellingly. The tamaracks talked to him, the poplars bowed as he passed, and the pines sang for him alone. The dying vines twined about his feet and clung to him, and the brown ferns, curling sadly, waved him a welcome that was a farewell. A bird twittered a plaintive note and a loon whistled a lonely call. Across the wide gray hollows and meadows of white moss moaned the north wind, bending all before it, blowing full into Siena's face with its bitter promise. The lichen-covered rocks and the rugged-barked trees and the creatures that moved among them—the whole world of earth and air heard Siena's step on the rustling leaves and a thousand voices hummed in the autumn stillness.

So he passed through the shadowy forest and over the gray muskeg flats to his hunting place. With his birchbark horn he blew the call of the moose. He alone of hunting Indians had the perfect moose call. There, hidden within a thicket, he waited, calling and listening till an angry reply bellowed from the depths of a hollow, and a bull moose, snorting fight, came cracking the saplings in his rush. When he sprang fierce and bristling into the glade, Siena killed him. Then, laying his shooting stick over a log, he drew his knife and approached the beast.

A snapping of twigs alarmed Siena and he whirled upon the defensive, but too late to save himself. A band of Indians pounced upon him and bore him to the ground. One wrestling heave Siena made, then he was overpowered and bound. Looking upward, he knew his captors, though he had never seen them before; they were the lifelong foes of his people, the fighting Crees.

A sturdy chief, bronze of face and sinister of eye, looked grimly down upon his captive. "Baroma makes Siena a slave."

Siena and his tribe were dragged far southward to the land of the Crees. The young chief was bound upon a block in the center of the village where hundreds of Crees spat upon him, beat him, and outraged him in every way their cunning could devise. Siena's gaze was on the north and his face showed no sign that he felt the torments.

At last Baroma's old advisers stopped the spectacle, saying: "This is a man!"

Siena and his people became slaves of the Crees. In Baroma's lodge, hung upon caribou antlers, was the wonderful shooting stick with Siena's powder horn and bullet pouch, objects of intense curiosity and fear.

None knew the mystery of this lightning-flashing, thunder-dealing thing; none dared touch it.

The heart of Siena was broken; not for his shattered dreams or the end of his freedom, but for his people. His fame had been their undoing. Slaves to the murderers of his forefathers! His spirit darkened, his soul sickened; no more did sweet voices sing to him on the wind, and his mind dwelt apart from his body among shadows and dim shapes.

Because of his strength he was worked like a dog at hauling packs and carrying wood; because of his fame he was set to cleaning fish and washing vessels with the squaws. Seldom did he get to speak a word to his mother or any of his people. Always he was driven.

One day, when he lagged almost fainting, a maiden brought him water to drink. Siena looked up, and all about him suddenly brightened, as when sunlight bursts from cloud.

"Who is kind to Siena?" he asked, drinking.

"Baroma's daughter," replied the maiden.

"What is her name?"

Quickly the maiden bent her head, veiling dusky eyes with dusky hair. "Emihiyah."

"Siena has wandered on lonely trails and listened to voices not meant for other ears. He has heard the music of Emihiyah on the winds. Let the daughter of Siena's great foe not fear to tell of her name."

"Emihiyah means a wind kiss on the flowers in the moonlight," she whispered shyly and fled.

Love came to the last of the Sienas and it was like a glory. Death shuddered no more in Siena's soul. He saw into the future, and out of his gloom he rose again, god chosen in his own sight, with such added beauty to his stern face and power to his piercing eye and strength to his lofty frame that the Crees quailed before him and marveled. Once more sweet voices came to him, and ever on the soft winds were songs of the dewy moorlands to the northward, songs of the pines and the laugh of the loon and of the rushing, green-white, thundering Athabasca, godforsaken river.

Siena's people saw him strong and patient, and they toiled on, unbroken, faithful. While he lived, the pride of Baroma was vaunting. "Siena waits" were the simple words he said to his mother, and she repeated them as wisdom. But the flame of his eye was like the leaping Northern Lights, and it kept alive the fire deep down in their breasts.

In the winter when the Crees lolled in their wigwams, when less labor fell to Siena, he set traps in the snow trails for silver fox and marten. No Cree had ever been such a trapper as Siena. In the long months he captured many furs, with which he wrought a robe the like of which had not before been the delight of a maiden's eye. He kept it by him for seven nights, and always during this time his ear was turned to the wind. The seventh night was the night of the midwinter feast, and when the torches burned bright in front of Baroma's lodge Siena took the robe and, passing slowly and stately till he stood before Emihiyah, he laid it at her feet.

Emihiyah's dusky face paled, her eyes that shone like stars drooped behind her flying hair, and all her slender body trembled.

"Slave!" cried Baroma, leaping erect. "Come closer that Baroma may see what kind of a dog approaches Emihiyah."

Siena met Baroma's gaze, but spoke no word. His gift spoke for him. The hated slave had dared to ask in marriage the hand of the proud Baroma's daughter. Siena towered in the firelight with something in his presence that for a moment awed beholders. Then the passionate and untried braves broke the silence with a clamor of the wolf pack.

Tillimanqua, wild son of Baroma, strung an arrow to his bow and shot it into Siena's hip, where it stuck, with feathered shaft quivering.

The spring of the panther was not swifter than Siena; he tossed Tillimanqua into the air and, flinging him down, trod on his neck and wrenched the bow away. Siena pealed out the long-drawn war whoop of his tribe that had not been heard for a hundred years, and the terrible cry stiffened the Crees in their tracks.

Then he plucked the arrow from his hip and, fitting it to the string, pointed the gory flint head at Tillimanqua's eyes and began to bend the bow. He bent the tough wood till the ends almost met, a feat of exceeding great strength, and thus he stood with brawny arms knotted and stretched.

A scream rent the suspense. Emihiyah fell upon her knees. "Spare Emihiyah's brother!"

Siena cast one glance at the kneeling maiden, then, twanging the bow string, he shot the arrow toward the sky.

"Baroma's slave is Siena," he said, with scorn like the lash of a whip. "Let the Cree learn wisdom."

Then Siena strode away, with a stream of dark blood down his thigh, and went to his brush tepee, where he closed his wound.

In the still watches of the night, when the stars blinked through the leaves and the dew fell, when Siena burned and throbbed in pain, a shadow passed between his weary eyes and the pale light. And a voice that was not one of the spirit voices on the wind called softly over him, "Siena! Emihiyah comes."

The maiden bound the hot thigh with a soothing balm and bathed his fevered brow.

Then her hands found his in tender touch, her dark face bent low to his, her hair lay upon his cheek. "Emihiyah keeps the robe," she said.

"Siena loves Emihiyah," he replied.

"Emihiyah loves Siena," she whispered.

She kissed him and stole away.

On the morrow Siena's wound was as if it had never been; no eye saw his pain. Siena returned to his work and his trapping. The winter melted into spring, spring flowered into summer, summer withered into autumn.

Once in the melancholy days Siena visited Baroma in his wigwam. "Baroma's hunters are slow. Siena sees a famine in the land."

"Let Baroma's slave keep his place among the squaws," was the reply.

That autumn the north wind came a moon before the Crees expected it; the reindeer took their annual march farther south; the moose herded warily in open groves; the whitefish did not run, and the seven-year pest depleted the rabbits.

When the first snow fell Baroma called a council and then sent his hunting braves far and wide.

One by one they straggled back to camp, footsore and hungry, and each with the same story. It was too late.

A few moose were in the forest, but they were wild and kept far out of range of the hunter's arrows, and there was no other game.

A blizzard clapped down upon the camp, and sleet and snow whitened the forest and filled the trails. Then winter froze everything in icy clutch. The old year drew to a close.

The Crees were on the brink of famine. All day and all night they kept up their chanting and incantations and beating of tom-toms to conjure the return of the reindeer. But no reindeer appeared.

It was then that the stubborn Baroma yielded to his advisers and consented to let Siena save them from starvation by means of his wonderful shooting stick. Accordingly Baroma sent word to Siena to appear at his wigwam.

Siena did not go, and said to the medicine men: "Tell Baroma soon it will be for Siena to demand."

Then the Cree chieftain stormed and stamped in his wigwam and swore away the life of his slave. Yet again the wise medicine men prevailed. Siena and the wonderful shooting stick would be the salvation of the Crees. Baroma, muttering deep in his throat like distant thunder, gave sentence to starve Siena until he volunteered to go forth to hunt, or let him be the first to die.

The last scraps of meat, except a little hoarded in Baroma's lodge, were devoured, and then began the boiling of bones and skins to make a soup to sustain life. The cold days passed and a silent gloom pervaded the camp. Sometimes a cry of a bereaved mother, mourning for a starved child, wailed through the darkness. Siena's people, long used to starvation, did not suffer or grow weak so soon as the Crees. They were of hardier frame, and they were upheld by faith in their chief. When he would sicken it would be time for them to despair. But Siena walked erect as in the days of his freedom, nor did he stagger under the loads of firewood, and there was a light on his face. The Crees, knowing of Baroma's order that Siena should be the first to perish of starvation, gazed at the slave first in awe, then in fear. The last of the Sienas was succored by the spirits.

But god-chosen though Siena deemed himself, he knew it was not by the spirits that he was fed in this time of famine. At night in the dead stillness, when even no mourning of wolf came over the frozen wilderness, Siena lay in his brush tepee close and warm under his blanket. The wind was faint and low, yet still it brought the old familiar voices. And it bore another sound—the soft fall of a moccasin on the snow. A shadow passed between Siena's eyes and the pale light.

"Emihiyah comes," whispered the shadow and knelt over him.

She tendered a slice of meat which she had stolen from Barorna's scant hoard as he muttered and growled in uneasy slumber. Every night since her father's order to starve Siena, Emihiyah had made this perilous errand.

And now her hand sought his and her dusky hair swept his brow. "Emihiyah is faithful," she breathed low.

"Siena only waits," he replied.

She kissed him and stole away.

Cruel days fell upon the Crees before Barorna's pride was broken. Many children died and some of the mothers were beyond help. Siena's people kept their strength, and he himself showed no effect of hunger. Long ago the Cree women had deemed him superhuman, that the Great Spirit fed him from the happy hunting grounds.

At last Baroma went to Siena. "Siena may save his people and the Crees."

Siena regarded him long, then replied: "Siena waits."

"Let Baroma know. What does Siena wait for? While he waits we die."

Siena smiled his slow, inscrutable smile and turned away.

Baroma sent for his daughter and ordered her to plead for her life.

Emihiyah came, fragile as a swaying reed, more beautiful than a rose choked in a tangled thicket, and she stood before Siena with doe eyes veiled. "Emihiyah begs Siena to save her and the tribe of Crees."

"Siena waits," replied the slave.

Baroma roared in his fury and bade his braves lash the slave. But the blows fell from feeble arms and Siena laughed at his captors.

Then, like a wild lion unleashed from long thrall, he turned upon them: "Starve! Cree dogs! Starve! When the Crees all fall like leaves in autumn, then Siena and his people will go back to the north."

Baroma's arrogance left him then, and on another day, when Emihiyah lay weak and pallid in his wigwam and the pangs of hunger gnawed at his own vitals, he again sought Siena. "Let Siena tell for what he waits."

Siena rose to his lofty height and the leaping flame of the Northern Light gathered in his eyes. "Freedom!" One word he spoke and it rolled away on the wind.

"Baroma yields," replied the Cree, and hung his head.

"Send the squaws who can walk and the braves who can crawl out upon Siena's trail."

Then Siena went to Baroma's lodge and took up the wonderful shooting stick and, loading it, he set out upon snowshoes into the white forest. He knew where to find the moose yards in the sheltered corners. He heard the bulls pounding the hard-packed snow and cracking their antlers on the trees. The wary beasts would not have allowed him to steal close, as a warrior armed with a bow must have done, but Siena fired into the herd at long range. And when they dashed off, sending the snow up like a spray, a huge black bull lay dead. Siena followed them as they floundered through the drifts, and whenever he came within range he shot again. When five moose were killed he turned upon his trail to find almost the whole Cree tribe had followed him and were tearing the meat and crying out in a kind of crazy joy. That night the fires burned before the wigwams, the earthen pots steamed, and there was great rejoicing. Siena hunted the next day, and the next, and for ten days he went into the white forest with his wonderful shooting stick, and eighty moose fell to his unerring aim.

The famine was broken and the Crees were saved.

When the mad dances ended and the feasts were over, Siena appeared before Baroma's lodge. "Siena will lead his people northward."

Baroma, starving, was a different chief from Baroma well fed and in no pain. All his cunning had returned. "Siena goes free. Baroma gave his word. But Siena's people remain slaves."

"Siena demanded freedom for himself and people," said the younger chief.

"Baroma heard no word of Siena's tribe. He would not have granted freedom for them. Siena's freedom was enough."

"The Cree twists the truth. He knows Siena would not go without his people. Siena might have remembered Baroma's cunning. The Crees were ever liars."

Baroma stalked before his fire with haughty presence. About him in the circle of light sat his medicine men, his braves and squaws. "The Cree is kind. He gave his word. Siena is free. Let him take his wonderful shooting stick and go back to the north."

Siena laid the shooting stick at Baroma's feet and likewise the powder horn and bullet pouch. Then he folded his arms, and his falcon eyes looked far beyond Baroma to the land of the changing lights and the old home on the green-white, rushing Athabasca, god-forsaken river. "Siena stays."

Baroma started in amaze and anger. "Siena makes Baroma's word idle. Begone!"

"Siena stays!"

The look of Siena, the pealing reply, for a moment held the chief mute. Slowly Baroma stretched wide his arms and lifted them, while from his face flashed a sullen wonder. "Great Slave!" he thundered.

So was respect forced from the soul of the Cree, and the name thus wrung from his jealous heart was one to live forever in the lives and legends of Siena's people.

Baroma sought the silence of his lodge, and his medicine men and braves dispersed, leaving Siena standing in the circle, a magnificent statue facing the steely north.

From that day insult was never offered to Siena, nor word spoken to him by the Crees, nor work given. He was free to come and go where he willed, and he spent his time in lessening the tasks of his people.

The trails of the forest were always open to him, as were the streets of the Cree village. If a brave met him, it was to step aside; if a squaw met him, it was to bow her head; if a chief met him, it was to face him as warriors faced warriors.

One twilight Emihiyah crossed his path, and suddenly she stood as once before, like a frail reed about to break in the wind. But Siena passed on. The days went by and each one brought less labor to Siena's people, until that one came wherein there was no task save what they set themselves. Siena's tribe were slaves, yet not slaves.

The winter wore by and the spring and the autumn, and again Siena's fame went abroad on the four winds. The Chippewayans journeyed from afar to see the Great Slave, and likewise the Blackfeet and the Yellow Knives. Honor would have been added to fame; councils called; overtures made to the somber Baroma on behalf of the Great Slave, but Siena passed to and fro among his people, silent and cold to all others, true to the place which his great foe had given him. Captive to a lesser chief, they said; the Great Slave who would yet free his tribe and gather to him a new and powerful nation.

Once in the late autumn Siena sat brooding in the twilight by Ema's tepee. That night all who came near him were silent. Again Siena was listening to voices on the wind, voices that had been still for long, which he had tried to forget. It was the north wind, and it whipped the spruces and moaned through the pines. In its cold breath it bore a message to Siena, a hint of coming winter and a call from

Naza, far north of the green-white, thundering Athabasca, river without a spirit.

In the darkness when the camp slumbered Siena faced the steely north. As he looked a golden shaft, arrow-shaped and arrow-swift, shot to the zenith.

"Naza!" he whispered to the wind. "Siena watches."

Then the gleaming, changing Northern Lights painted a picture of gold and silver bars, of flushes pink as shell, of opal fire and sunset red; and it was a picture of Siena's life from the moment the rushing Athabasca rumbled his name, to the far distant time when he would say farewell to his great nation and pass forever to the retreat of the winds. God chosen he was, and had power to read the story in the sky.

Seven nights Siena watched in the darkness; and on the seventh night, when the golden flare and silver shafts faded in the north, he passed from tepee to tepee, awakening his people. "When Siena's people hear the sound of the shooting stick let them cry greatly: Siena kills Baroma! Siena kills Baroma!"

With noiseless stride Siena went among the wigwams and along the lanes until he reached Baroma's lodge. Entering in the dark he groped with his hands upward to a moose's antlers and found the shooting stick. Outside he fired it into the air.

Like a lightning bolt the report ripped asunder the silence, and the echoes clapped and reclapped from the cliffs. Sharp on the dying echoes Siena bellowed his war whoop, and it was the second time in a hundred years for foes to hear that terrible, long-drawn cry.

Then followed the shrill yells of Siena's people: "Siena kills Baroma...Siena kills Baroma...Siena kills Baroma!"

The slumber of the Crees awoke to a babel of many voices; it rose hoarsely on the night air, swelled hideously into a deafening roar that shook the earth.

In this din of confusion and terror when the Crees were lamenting the supposed death of Baroma and screaming in each other's ears, "The Great Slave takes his freedom!" Siena ran to his people and, pointing to the north, drove them before him.

Single file, like a long line of flitting specters, they passed out of the fields into the forest. Siena kept close on their trail, ever looking backward, and ready with the shooting stick.

The roar of the stricken Crees softened in his ears and at last died away.

Under the black canopy of whispering leaves, over the gray, mist-shrouded muskeg flats, around the glimmering reed-bordered ponds, Siena drove his people.

All night Siena hurried them northward and with every stride his heart beat higher. Only he was troubled by a sound like the voice that came to him on the wind.

But the wind was now blowing in his face, and the sound appeared to be at his back. It followed on his trail as had the step of destiny. When he strained his ears he could not hear it, yet when he had gone on swiftly, persuaded it was only fancy, then the voice that was not a voice came haunting him.

In the gray dawn Siena halted on the far side of a gray flat and peered through the mists on his back trail. Something moved out among the shadows, a gray shape that crept slowly, uttering a mournful cry.

"Siena is trailed by a wolf," muttered the chief.

Yet he waited, and saw that the wolf was an Indian. He raised the fatal shooting stick.

As the Indian staggered forward, Siena recognized the robe of silver fox and marten, his gift to Emihiyah. He laughed in mockery. It was a Cree trick. Tillimanqua had led the pursuit disguised in his sister's robe. Baroma would find his son dead on the Great Slave's trail.

"Siena!" came the strange, low cry.

It was the cry that had haunted him like the voice on the wind. He leaped as a bounding deer.

Out of the gray fog burned dusky eyes half-veiled by dusky hair, and little hands that he knew wavered as fluttering leaves. "Emihiyah comes," she said.

"Siena waits," he replied.

Out of the gray fog burned dusky eyes half veiled by dusky hair–"Emihiyah comes," she said. "Siena waits," he replied.

Far to the northward he led his bride and his people, far beyond the old home on the green-white, thundering Athabasca, god-forsaken river; and there, on the lonely shores of an inland sea, he fathered the Great Slave Tribe.

WINE IN THE DESERT

Max Brand

There was no hurry, except for the thirst, like clotted salt, in the back of his throat, and Durante rode on slowly, rather enjoying the last moments of dryness before he reached the cold water in Tony's house. There was really no hurry at all. He had almost twenty-four hours' head start, for they would not find his dead man until this morning. After that, there would be perhaps several hours of delay before the sheriff gathered a sufficient posse and started on his trail. Or perhaps the sheriff would be fool enough to come alone.

Durante had been able to see the wheel and fan of Tony's windmill for more than an hour, but he could not make out the ten acres of the vineyard until he had topped the last rise, for the vines had been planted in a hollow. The lowness of the ground, Tony used to say, accounted for the water that gathered in the well during the wet season. The rains sank through the desert sand, through the gravels beneath, and gathered in a bowl of clay hardpan far below.

In the middle of the rainless season the well ran dry but, long before that, Tony had every drop of the water pumped up into a score of tanks made of cheap corrugated iron. Slender pipe lines carried the water from the tanks to the vines and from time to time let them sip enough life to keep them until the winter darkened overhead suddenly, one November day, and the rain came down, and all the earth made a great hushing sound as it drank. Durante had heard that whisper of drinking when he was here before; but he never had seen the place in the middle of the long drought.

The windmill looked like a sacred emblem to Durante, and the twenty stodgy, tar-painted tanks blessed his eyes; but a heavy sweat broke out at once from his body. For the air of the hollow, unstirred by wind, was hot and still as a bowl of soup. A reddish soup. The vines were powdered with thin red dust, also. They were wretched, dying things to look at, for the grapes had been gathered, the new wine had been made, and now the leaves hung in ragged tatters.

Durante rode up to the squat adobe house and right through the entrance into the patio. A flowering vine clothed three sides on the little court. Durante did not know the name of the plant, but it had large white blossoms with golden hearts that poured sweetness on the air. Durante hated the sweetness. It made him more thirsty.

He threw the reins of his mule and strode into the house. The water cooler stood in the hall outside the kitchen. There were two jars made of a porous stone, very ancient things, and the liquid which distilled through the pores kept the contents cool. The jar on the left held water; that on the right contained wine. There was a big tin dipper hanging on a peg beside each jar. Durante tossed off the cover of the vase on the left and plunged it in until the delicious coolness closed well above his wrist.

"Hey, Tony," he called. Out of his dusty throat the cry was a mere groaning. He drank and called again, clearly, "Tony!"

A voice pealed from the distance.

Durante, pouring down the second dipper of water, smelled the alkali dust which had shaken off his own clothes. It seemed to him that heat was radiating like light from his clothes, from his body, and the cool dimness of the house was soaking it up. He heard the wooden leg of Tony bumping on the ground, and Durante grinned; then Tony came in with that hitch and sideswing with which he accommodated the stiffness of his artificial leg. His brown face shone with sweat as though a special ray of light were focused on it.

"Ah, Dick!" he said. "Good old Dick!... How long since you came last!... Wouldn't Julia be glad! Wouldn't she be glad!"

"Ain't she here?" asked Durante, jerking his head suddenly away from the dripping dipper.

"She's away at Nogalez," said Tony. "It gets so hot. I said, 'You go up to Nogalez, Julia, where the wind don't forget to blow.' She cried, but I made her go."

"Did she cry?" asked Durante.

"Julia... that's a good girl," said Tony.

"Yeah. You bet she's good," said Durante. He put the dipper quickly to his lips but did not swallow for a moment; he was grinning too widely. Afterward he said: "You wouldn't throw some water into that mule of mine, would you, Tony?"

Tony went out with his wooden leg clumping loud on the wooden floor, softly in the patio dust. Durante found the hammock in the corner of the patio. He lay down in it and watched the color of sunset flush the mists of desert dust that rose to the zenith. The water was soaking through his body; hunger began, and then the rattling of pans in the kitchen and the cheerful cry of Tony's voice:

"What you want, Dick? I got some pork. You don't want pork. I'll make you some good Mexican beans. Hot. Ah ha, I know that old Dick. I have plenty of good wine for you, Dick. Tortillas. Even Julia can't make tortillas like me... And what about a nice young rabbit?"

"All blowed full of buckshot?" growled Durante.

"No, no. I kill them with the rifle."

"You kill rabbits with a rifle?" repeated Durante, with a quick interest.

"It's the only gun I have," said Tony. "If I catch them in the sights, they are dead... A wooden leg cannot walk very far... I must kill them quick. You see? They come close to the house about sunrise and flop their ears. I shoot through the head."

"Yeah? Yeah?" muttered Durante. "Through the head?" He relaxed, scowling. He passed his hand over his face, over his head.

Then Tony began to bring the food out into the patio and lay it on a small wooden table; a lantern hanging against the wall of the house included the table in a dim half circle of light. They sat there and ate. Tony had scrubbed himself for the meal. His hair was soaked in water and sleeked back over his round skull. A man in the desert might be willing to pay five dollars for as much water as went to the soaking of that hair.

Everything was good. Tony knew how to cook, and he knew how to keep the glasses filled with his wine.

"This is old wine. This is my father's wine. Eleven years old," said Tony. "You look at the light through it. You see that brown in the red? That's the soft that time puts in good wine, my father always said."

"What killed your father?" asked Durante.

Tony lifted his hand as though he were listening or as though he were pointing out a thought.

"The desert killed him. I found his mule. It was dead, too. There was a leak in the canteen. My father was only five miles away when the buzzards showed him to me."

"Five miles? Just an hour... Good Lord!" said Durante. He stared with big eyes. "Just dropped down and died?" he asked.

"No," said Tony. "When you die of thirst, you always die just one way... First you tear off your shirt, then your undershirt. That's to be cooler... And the sun comes and cooks your bare skin... And then you think... there is water everywhere, if you dig down far enough. You begin to dig. The dust comes up your nose. You start screaming. You break your nails in the sand. You wear the flesh off the tips of your fingers, to the bone." He took a quick swallow of wine.

"Without you seen a man die of thirst, how d'you know they start to screaming?" asked Durante.

"They got a screaming look when you find them," said Tony. "Take some more wine. The desert never can get to you here. My father showed me the way to keep the desert away from the hollow. We live pretty good here? No?"

"Yeah," said Durante, loosening his shirt collar. "Yeah, pretty good."

Afterward he slept well in the hammock until the report of a rifle waked him and he saw the color of dawn in the sky. It was such a great, round bowl that for a moment he felt as though he were above, looking down into it.

He got up and saw Tony coming in holding a rabbit by the ears, the rifle in his other hand.

"You see?" said Tony. "Breakfast came and called on us!" He laughed.

Durante examined the rabbit with care. It was nice and fat and it had been shot through the head. Through the middle of the head. Such a shudder went down the back of Durante that he washed gingerly before breakfast; he felt that his blood was cooled for the entire day.

It was a good breakfast, too, with flapjacks and stewed rabbit with green peppers, and a quart of strong coffee. Before they had finished, the sun struck through the east window and started them sweating.

"Gimme a look at that rifle of yours, Tony, will you?" Durante asked.

"You take a look at my rifle, but don't you steal the luck that's in it," laughed Tony. He brought the fifteen-shot Winchester.

"Loaded right to the brim?" asked Durante.

"I always load it full the minute I get back home," said Tony.

"Tony, come outside with me," commanded Durante.

They went out from the house. The sun turned the sweat of Durante to hot water and then dried his skin so that his clothes felt transparent.

"Tony, I gotta be damn mean," said Durante. "Stand right there where I can see you. Don't try to get close... Now listen... The sheriff's gunna be along this trail some-time today, looking for me. He'll load up himself and all his gang with water out of your tanks. Then he'll follow my sign across the desert. Get me? He'll follow if he finds water on the place. But he's not gunna find water."

"What you done, poor Dick?" said Tony. "Now look... I could hide you in the old wine cellar where nobody..."

"The sheriff's not gunna find any water," said Durante. "It's gunna be like this."

He put the rifle to his shoulder, aimed, fired. The shot struck the base of the nearest tank, ranging down through the bottom. A semicircle of darkness began to stain the soil near the edge of the iron wall.

Tony fell on his knees. "No, no, Dick! Good Dick!" he said. "Look! All the vineyard. It will die. It will turn into old, dead wood. Dick..."

"Shut your face," said Durante. "Now I've started, I kinda like the job."

Tony fell on his face and put his hands over his ears. Durante drilled a bullet hole through the tanks, one after another. Afterward, he leaned on the rifle.

"Take my canteen and go in and fill it with water out of the cooling jar," he said. "Snap into it, Tony!"

Tony got up. He raised the canteen and looked around him, not at the tanks from which the water was pouring so that the noise of the earth drinking was audible, but at the rows of his vineyard. Then he went into the house.

Durante mounted his mule. He shifted the rifle to his left hand and drew out the heavy Colt from its holster. Tony came dragging back to him, his head down. Durante watched Tony with a careful revolver but he gave up the canteen without lifting his eyes.

"The trouble with you, Tony," said Durante, "is you're yellow. I'd of fought a tribe of wildcats with my bare hands before I'd let 'em do what I'm doin' to you. But you sit back and take it."

Tony did not seem to hear. He stretched out his hands to the vines.

"Ah, my God," said Tony. "Will you let them all die?"

Durante shrugged his shoulders. He shook the canteen to make sure that it was full. It was so brimming that there was hardly room for the liquid to make a sloshing sound. Then he turned the mule and kicked it into a dogtrot.

Half a mile from the house of Tony, he threw the empty rifle to the ground. There was no sense packing that useless weight, and Tony with his peg leg would hardly come this far.

Durante looked back, a mile or so later, and saw the little image of Tony picking up the rifle from the dust, then staring earnestly after his guest. Durante remembered the neat little hole clipped through the head of the rabbit. Wherever he went, his trail never could return again to the vineyard in the desert. But then, commencing to picture to himself the arrival of the sweating sheriff and his posse at the house of Tony, Durante laughed heartily.

The sheriff's posse could get plenty of wine, of course, but without water a man could not hope to make the desert voyage, even with a mule or a horse to help him on the way. Durante patted the full, rounding side of his canteen. He might even now begin with the first sip but it was a luxury to postpone pleasure until desire became greater.

He raised his eyes along the trail. Close by, it was merely dotted with occasional bones, but distance joined the dots into an unbroken chalk line which wavered with a strange leisure across the Apache Desert, pointing toward the cool blue promise of the mountains. The next morning he would be among them.

A coyote whisked out of a gully and ran like a gray puff of dust on the wind. His tongue hung out like a little red rag from the side of his mouth; and suddenly Durante was dry to the marrow. He uncorked and lifted his canteen. It had a slightly sour smell; perhaps the sacking which covered it had grown a trifle old. And then he poured a great mouthful of lukewarm liquid. He had swallowed it before his senses could give him warning.

It was wine.

He looked first of all toward the mountains. They were as calmly blue, as distant as when he had started that morning. Twenty-four hours not on water, but on wine.

"I deserve it," said Durante. "I trusted him to fill the canteen... I deserve it. Curse him!"

With a mighty resolution, he quieted the panic in his soul. He would not touch the stuff until noon. Then he would take one discreet sip. He would win through.

Hours went by. He looked at his watch and found it was only ten o'clock. And he had thought that it was on the verge of noon! He uncorked the wine and drank freely and, corking the canteen, felt almost as though he needed a drink of water more than before. He sloshed the contents of the canteen. Already it was horribly light.

Once, he turned the mule and considered the return trip; but he could remember the head of the rabbit too clearly, drilled right through the center. The vineyard, the rows of old twisted, gnarled little trunks with the bark peeling off... every vine was to Tony like a human life. And Durante had condemned them all to death.

He faced the blue of the mountains again. His heart raced in his breast with terror. Perhaps it was fear and not the suction of that dry and deadly air that made his tongue cleave to the roof of his mouth.

The day grew old. Nausea began to work in his stomach, nausea alternating with sharp pains. When he looked down, he saw that there was blood on his boots. He had been spurring the mule until the red ran down from its flanks. It went with a curious stagger, like a rocking horse with a broken rocker; and Durante grew aware that he had been keeping the mule at a gallop for a long time. He pulled it to a halt. It stood with wide-braced legs. Its head was down. When he leaned from the saddle, he saw that its mouth was open.

"It's gunna die," said Durante. "It's gunna die... what a fool I been..."

The mule did not die until after sunset. Durante left everything except his revolver. He packed the weight of that for an hour and discarded it, in turn. His knees were growing weak. When he looked up at the stars, they shone white and clear for a moment only, and then whirled into little racing circles and scrawls of red.

He lay down. He kept his eyes closed and waited for the shaking to go out of his body, but it would not stop. And every breath of darkness was like an inhalation of black dust.

He got up and went on, staggering. Sometimes he found himself running.

Before you die of thirst, you go mad. He kept remembering that. His tongue had swollen big. Before it choked him, if he lanced it with his knife the blood would help him; he would be able to swallow. Then he remembered that the taste of blood is salty.

Once, in his boyhood, he had ridden through a pass with his father and they had looked down on the sapphire of a mountain lake, a hundred thousand million tons of water as cold as snow...

When he looked up, now, there were no stars; and this frightened him terribly. He never had seen a desert night so dark. His eyes were failing, he was being blinded. When the morning came, he would not be able to see the mountains, and he would walk around and around in a circle until he dropped and died.

No stars, no wind; the air as still as the waters of a stale pool, and he in the dregs at the bottom...

He seized his shirt at the throat and tore it away so that it hung in two rags from his hips.

He could see the earth only well enough to stumble on the rocks. But there were no stars in the heavens. He was blind: he had no more hope than a rat in a well. Ah, but Italian devils know how to put poison in wine that steal all the senses or any one of them: and Tony had chosen to blind Durante.

He heard a sound like water. It was the swishing of the soft deep sand through which he was treading; sand so soft that a man could dig it away with his bare hands...

Afterward, after many hours, out of the blind face of that sky the rain began to fall. It made first a whispering and then a delicate murmur like voices conversing, but after that, just at the dawn, it roared like the hoofs of ten thousand charging horses. Even through that thundering confusion the big birds with naked heads and red, raw necks found their way down to one place in the Apache Desert.

AUTHORS

JACK LONDON was born John Griffith Chaney on January 12, 1876, in San Francisco, California. After working in the Klondike, London returned home and began publishing stories. His novels, including The Call of the Wild, White Fang and Martin Eden, placed London among the most popular American authors of his time. London, who was also a journalist and an outspoken socialist, died in 1916.

PEARL ZANE GREY (January 31, 1872 - October 23, 1939) was an American author and dentist best known for his popular adventure novels and stories associated with the Western genre in literature and the arts; he idealized the American frontier.

FRANCIS BRETT HART (August 25, 1836[1] - May 5, 1902), known as Bret Harte, was an American short-story writer and poet, best remembered for his short fiction featuring miners, gamblers, and other romantic figures of the California Gold Rush.

STEPHEN CRANE (November 1, 1871 - June 5, 1900) was an American poet, novelist, and short story writer. Prolific throughout his short life, he wrote notable works in the Realist tradition as well as early examples of American Naturalism and Impressionism. He is recognized by modern critics as one of the most innovative writers of his generation.

WILLA SIBERT CATHER (December 7, 1873 - April 24, 1947) was an American writer who achieved recognition for her novels of frontier life on the Great Plains, including O Pioneers! (1913), The Song of the Lark (1915), and My Ántonia (1918). In 1923 she was awarded the Pulitzer Prize for One of Ours (1922), a novel set during World War I.

WILLIAM SYDNEY PORTER (born William Sidney Porter, September 11, 1862 - June 5, 1910), better known by his pen name O. Henry, was an American short story writer. His stories are known for their surprise endings.

FREDERICK SCHILLER FAUST (May 29, 1892 - May 12, 1944) was an American author known primarily for his thoughtful and literary Westerns under the pen name Max Brand. Faust (as Max Brand) also created the popular fictional character of young medical intern Dr. James Kildare in a series of pulp fiction stories.

Printed in the USA
CPSIA information can be obtained
at www.ICGtesting.com
LVHW081833071123
763293LV00011B/1085

9 786589 575191